CREATIVE WRITING FROM NORTH WEST ENGLAND

Edited by Liz Wakefield

First published in Great Britain in 2002 by
YOUNG WRITERS
Remus House,
Coltsfoot Drive,
Peterborough, PE2 9JX
Telephone (01733) 890066

HB ISBN 0 75432 784 1
SB ISBN 0 75432 785 X

FOREWORD

This year Young Writers proudly presents a showcase of the best 'Days Of Our Lives . . .' short stories, from up-and-coming writers nationwide.

To write a short story is a difficult exercise. We made it more challenging by setting the theme of 'A Day In The Life Of Someone From The Second Millennium', using no more than 250 words! Much imagination and skill is required. *Days Of Our Lives . . . Creative Writing From North West England* achieves and exceeds these requirements. This exciting anthology will not disappoint the reader.

The thought, effort, imagination and hard work put into each story impressed us all, and again, the task of editing proved demanding due to the quality of entries received, but was nevertheless enjoyable.

We hope you are as pleased as we are with the final selection and that you continue to enjoy *Days Of Our Lives . . . Creative Writing From North West England* for many years to come.

CONTENTS

Middlewich Primary School

Vernon Junior School

Weaver Primary School

Yew Tree Primary School

The Stories

A DAY IN THE LIFE OF PICASSO

June 16th 1952

Last night I dreamt that I'd become more famous than I already am. I love drawing and painting but I'm not sure if people understand or even like my paintings for what they are. People do not understand how difficult it is to paint.

Today I'm going to meet my friends at the cafe. We will talk about what paintings we have done since we last saw each other.

One of my favourite pictures is a sleeping woman, it's a great picture. It's such a shame that nobody likes it. After all that hard work, I might just not bother. Well of course musicians, the people next door obviously thought it was a piece of music.

You wouldn't believe this, I've forgotten the cafe I go to after all these years, at least I know it's French. You see this other mate of mine wants to find out the name of it so he and his boss can go there. All I could say about it is that it's a nice French place. That obviously shows that I'm getting on in years. Phew, I wish I was eighteen again. That's all for now and goodnight.

Francesca Hoare (10)
All Saints RC Primary School

A Day In The Life Of Alexander Graham Bell

10th March 1876

It was 8am in the morning and I was having breakfast, it was a sunny day as the sun was streaming through the glass windows. After breakfast I went up my creaking stairs to get changed.

At 9am I was in the lab sorting out equipment for the experiment Mr Watson and I were doing, which I hope is going to work. For our experiment we need a glass box, a cork and brass ribbon and then we have to connect them together. After we connected them together Mr Watson went into another room, so I thought I would try the experiment out again. I put my face into the water and spoke, lots of bubbles came out of my mouth as I spoke.

Suddenly Mr Watson came out of the room, as I looked at his face he said, 'I heard and understood the words that you said.'
We both looked at each other in amazement.

I went straight to tell a colleague about the wonderful news. When I got to my colleague's house I told him what happened, my colleague asked me if I would like to sit down, so I did. Then we carried on talking. When I got closer to the good news I started to slow down. Suddenly the news spat out of my big mouth.
I looked at my colleague, I said, 'Don't you think that's good?'
He didn't say anything because he was so shocked.

Cally Bainbridge (9)
All Saints RC Primary School

A Day In The Life Of An Egyptian

After lunch, I was walking into the dressing room to get ready for the next dance for the king. I came across a very nice dress. I looked around to ask if I could wear the beautiful dress but no one was about so I looked at the dress, it had tons of gold on it, I couldn't believe my eyes. I had come across a lovely silver badge, now, I couldn't wear it, it would not only be rude as it wasn't mine, it was such a rare dress, so I put it back.

Suddenly as I was getting changed there was a scream from the princess. I quickly put my wig on and ran to her.
'Your Majesty,' I cried, 'I heard . . .'
Right in front of me was a dirty robber holding the royal family back in chains!
'How . . ?' I blurted out.

About nine men came and pushed me down, one started whipping me, I screamed.
'You killed all the Jewish children.' Shouted the man who whipped me.
'No father did.' The princess mumbled.

He got a knife out of his pocket and put its cold blade against my neck. The man swished the knife. I quickly grabbed the knife, punched him and hurried the princess away from harm. I'm going to pray to the gods.

Nicola Wareing (10)
All Saints RC Primary School

A Day In The Life Of An Ant

8am
Busy getting my little sister ready for school. It is a bit like an ant carrying food on its shiny, black back.

8.50am
The bell rings and there are lots of children hurrying into their classrooms. Just like little ants scuttling into the plants to collect food for the cold, bitter winter.

10.30am
Time for a quick break before we go back to the hard, hot work. It is very tiring in the hot sun working all day.

12.15am
Time to eat some of the yummy food we have collected to last us through the cold and bitter winters. We have collected a lot of food. We have collected enough food so we can have it everyday but only little.

3.30pm
Time to go home but there is a lot more work to do tomorrow.

8pm
Time to go to bed because you have to get a lot of sleep for the day ahead. It is the same everyday but we sometimes collect different food. I am really tired . . . wait, what is that, oh no it is a giant purple plum rolling towards me. It must be the food we collected.

9pm
It is coming at me and there is another peace of fruit, a yellow, curved banana. Oops . . . I didn't put them on properly. They put the light on . . . phew! It was only you. You're good at scaring people, oops, I mean ants.

Katheryn McCambridge (9)
All Saints RC Primary School

A DAY IN THE LIFE OF DAVID BECKHAM

I had a busy morning today. I got up at 6am and headed out from my home in Alderly Edge, to the training centre in Carrington. I spent a few hours training, doing sit-ups and having a game with the lads. Then I went for a swim. I did ten lengths to keep me fit.

At 12pm I left Carrington and went to pick up Victoria and Brooklyn. We then went to Handforth Dean and had our lunch at John Lewis! Brooklyn was really good so I bought him a pair of trainers. You never know, he might be a singing footballer.

On the way home I couldn't believe it, but I got stopped for speeding. The policeman let me off though, I said a fan was chasing me. We called to see Gary and Julie Neville and then we went home to watch a Spice Girl video.

Victoria prepared the tea. Soon it was time to get changed for our match, United against Newcastle. I got in the car and went to the match. The final score was 2-0 to us. Then I went to the changing rooms, got changed and went home.

Calum Cummins (10)
All Saints RC Primary School

A Day In The Life Of A Caveman

I woke up on the rocky floor of my cave, the thunder and lightning spread over the sky. The howling wind whistled through the cracks of the walls. As I got up the lightning lit up the room and I could see my way through the dark. I knew that it was going to be a miserable day once again.

Quickly I pulled more bear skins over me to keep out the sharp, icy wind. Hunger pains tore through my stomach as I crammed some berries in my mouth and the juice trickled down my beard. I knew berries wouldn't last me a whole day so I would have to go hunting.

I started to walk through the damp forest floor looking both ways to see if there was a wild boar or deer. My tummy began to grumble fiercely now and again. I knew I could hear a sound so I went to see what it was. In front of me was a boar so I whacked it around the head and dragged it back to my cave. In my cave I started to eat but I was getting tired so I left the rest and went to my skins and fell asleep.

Thomas Christon (10)
All Saints RC Primary School

A DAY IN THE LIFE OF A BUMBLEBEE

As I woke up this morning a sweet scent came drifting to my attention, so I got up and followed the divine smell. As the smell got nearer and nearer, I started to approach a beautiful garden with lovely flowers everywhere. I decided to go to the fragrant roses, so I sniffed my nose right into the roses. Mmmm. I thought as I ate the scrumptious nectar. Well I thought that's breakfast over.

I flew back home to have a little rest but soon I was back out after a few hours for my lunch. I buzzed my wings in every direction till suddenly I found flowers much sweeter than before, so I flew my wings as fast as I could towards them. Bang! I hit something hard, it must have been protecting the flowers. I tried again but I still hit it. Then I noticed a giant thing entering it so I followed it and suddenly I was inside. The giant was watering the scrumptious flower, so I went to try the nectar but I was hit hard by a giant thing with five sticks hanging out of it. I was totally outraged, so I pointed my tail and stuck it into the five sticked hand. Then as the figure ran away I quickly grabbed some nectar, it was delicious.

Ouch, I thought, I was feeling rather sick, suddenly, my eyes flashed before me and I was dead.

Fiona Stuart (10)
All Saints RC Primary School

A DAY IN THE LIFE OF AN ANT

I woke up, then crawled out from under my brick house, then peered around. No one was out yet but it was that dreaded day, known to all ants as 'the birthday'. I remember it clearly from last year. Five or six humans charge around for two hours. It was the 27th July.

Then a body darted out, the party was about to start. A ball was thumped in my direction. I quickly dodged it. A giant rushed at me, I froze, as if my spine had snapped and luckily it missed me.

I crawled onto the patio, away from the 'destructors'. Then something flew out of a high window. I dashed for my life. It rattled on the ground. It was what they call 'pen' or 'biro'. I scuttled to the rockery to watch the ball zoom around. It was getting dark, I might survive the birthday party again. I jumped down off the rockery to eat some grass. I nibbled away for five minutes. Then I looked up. What! I thought, they've gone! I'd survived a second birthday party I'd witnessed. I danced around the patio for half an hour. All of a sudden I lost my footing and slipped down a crack. I had one hand hanging on for dear life. I heaved myself up. I decided to be a little more careful and crept back inside my brickhouse. What an eventful, scary and action-packed day. A year of worrying about the next birthday is about to begin.

Sean Zurawski (10)
All Saints RC Primary School

A DAY IN THE LIFE OF LIBBY

It was a beautiful morning, I stretched out on my bed. I had my breakfast first and when I saw that basket I thought, 'Oh no, I am going to the vets'.

I ran up the stairs as fast as I could and Alma shouted at me, she got me and put me in the basket and I couldn't stop miaowing all the way there. So Alma rang the bell and the vet opened the door to let Alma in and when it was my turn I thought, 'Oh no, oh no, this is bad'.

The vet got me out of the basket, he put me on the table and I had to have a needle in me and I miaowed again because I thought it was going to hurt me.

The vet said to Alma, 'Could you just turn her head towards you please,' so Alma did and when he did it, it didn't hurt one bit.

Then Sally and Vicky and Karen came to see me and after when they had gone, I popped my head out of the gate and then I went in and had something to eat.

Vicky Young (10)
All Saints RC Primary School

THE LIFE OF A HAMSTER

I am a golden hamster, I come from the rodent group of mammals. I sleep in the day and I come out at night, full of life. I can come out and travel up to twenty kilometres a night.

I easily bite if I am not handled right. I do not like it when people squeeze me and I don't like it when people trap me in my ball.

People need to keep on putting their hands out so I can keep on running without falling off. I eat lots of nuts every night. I sometimes get a treat like grapes, apple or cheese.

I need to be healthy, my eyes need to be bright and clear, nose clean and mouth clean in case of any problems, my coat well groomed.

I usually stay in my house until 8.00 and I come out about 10.00 when nobody is out. Some people put chew sticks in my cage and I really like them.

People buy me a ball so I can run around the house and get lots of exercise. Some people buy me a sharp stone that goes in my cage, I sharpen my teeth on it, they also put in my cage a stone strawberry.

Adam Cross (9)
All Saints RC Primary School

A Day In The Life Of An Ant

Yesterday I went to the watering hole when I got there I was shocked to find that the hole was empty, not a drop in it, I ran one metre back to the ant hill and told the queen. She asked for the fastest runner, he could run two miles a day. He went to make sure I was not bluffing to the queen, he came back and said, 'He was not bluffing.' The queen called for the strongest army to look for water they came back three whole hours later and they had found a huge pond with one litre of water in it with some small animals that can swim in it. The queen sent a new refreshed army with buckets to gather water from the pond. They came back in two hours because they were very refreshed and the water was in their buckets, made of leaves in a cone shape.

Later that day we grew some crops only the crop was called cress and grew very fast. We made the most crops ever that day.

Ben Glenny (9)
All Saints RC Primary School

THE LIFE OF A WORM

I woke up and saw a swaying leaf, 'Scrumptious,' I thought.

I squiddled across as quickly as my slithery pink body could carry me.
Just when I was about to take the first bite Joe the gardener stood on
me, it did hurt but I've got cold blood so I rushed over to the leaf and
munched it down, delicious, I thought to myself.

. . . Then I rushed off to a piece of dirt and started digging a new house I
saw a few friends when digging, like Jo-Jo and Jon-Jon. We all started
digging again, five minutes later we took a quick rest then we finished. I
ran home passing many leaves, scrumptious, I thought.

I was about to take the first bite when the tree fell down. Doh! I
thought, then my mum called me for tea. I slithered like Linford
Christie but faster.

The minute I got in I saw my favourite leaves and grass, and then for
pudding my tummy was rumbling. So I went in the garden to find some
food. I saw the best leaf, just when I was about to take the first bite,
'Squash!'

Michael Gleave (9)
All Saints RC Primary School

A Day In The Life Of An Ant

It's sunrise and my room is filled with a beautiful glow. I can't wait to hunt for jam because my stomach has been growling ever since I woke up. It's not fair at all. I'm the smallest one so I don't get to hunt by myself. I'll show them.

I smelt some jam nearby, eventually I set off to find out where the beautiful smell was coming from. I lingered off slowly, still half asleep, into the forest, but suddenly my dad called me.

'Don't go to the jam, it's a trick. Aunty Don told me that the humans want to put ants in a jar,' he shouted.

'I'm going to go, to show you that I'm not a baby anymore,' I replied.

The trees made a loud swishing noise as I saw the sun glistening in the sky.

I got closer to the jam, then suddenly thump. I got trapped in an exceedingly small jar, and I didn't know what to do.

I twisted and turned and I finally got out because my clever eye spotted a hole.

The boy that put me in the house had gone out to play so I crawled home.

Unfortunately it was bedtime. Today I learnt that I must *always* listen to my parents.

Lilian Lau (10)
All Saints RC Primary School

AN ANT'S LIFE

Dear Diary

I woke up feeling refreshed. I could feel the light breeze on my head and I sat on my bed for a few minutes. I could tell something was going to happen today, something very soon too. I came into the kitchen and started to eat my breakfast. Mother said, 'Hello dear, sleep well? What are you doing today?'
I replied, 'Yes, I did and nothing much.'

'That's not like you Christina,' she said,
'Suppose,' I sighed.

As I walked to school I heard a cry for help, I ran towards the forest wondering if an ant had got trapped! I ran in just in time to take him home.

I grabbed her, ran for the exit, a red ant came up in front of us and I tried to pass him, but he was a feisty one. We finally got past him, he was a red warrior, I replied, 'I'm a black warrior.'

We made it to the hospital and I had missed school. But I think it was worth it, to save a antling in trouble, in the forest. I think though, I'm in a lot of trouble with my mum, she is going to ground me.

I also think this is my longest diary piece, oh! And the little antling is OK so I'm happy.

Christina Dykes (10)
All Saints RC Primary School

THE DAY IN THE LIFE AS A MINIBEAST

On the 17th May 2001, I was walking down the hard wet sand with the waves splashing at my face, then suddenly . . . I spotted a big house with footprints above the beach on a hill. I didn't know if I should go in or run away, I don't know what made me but I chose to go in. I slowly crept towards the house, I opened the door a person shouted 'Arrgh!'

'I didn't know what was wrong,' they said, 'I'd got a little hairy face,' I said, 'I know because I am a minibeast.' She was scared of me but we finally made friends.

She lived there, I told her I lived in a hole on a hill. I told her I saw her footprints and so I followed them.

Suddenly . . . a storm came, the sea was like an angry dog crashing against the rocks. We all went inside to a safer place until the storm broke.

When the sun came out again we went out and had a walk along the beach. The waves were splashing against us and the sand was hard against our feet and the shells went deep in the sand when we stood on them. It got darker and darker so we decided to go home. I said I travelled all around the world and tomorrow I was leaving for a new place, so that night I went to my hole. In the morning I went to Laura's house, I said my first and last goodbye and waved, then I flew away.

Rebecca Wilson (10)
All Saints RC Primary School

A Day In The Life Of Sir Isaac Newton

I woke this morning thinking of something to do for the day, then I had an idea, I would do an experiment on gravity. I would climb and climb right to the top of the Leaning Tower of Pisa and drop a penny and a feather.

So I got up and had my breakfast, got ready and went to the Leaning Tower of Pisa with a penny and a feather I climbed and climbed until I reached the top, there was a big crowd , I dropped them together and at the same time they both hit the ground at the same time. Everyone was shocked because they were wrong. I went home and had dinner in a very happy mood. I watched TV and went to bed.

Sarah Glenny (10)
All Saints RC Primary School

A Day In The Life Of Zac The Dog

When I woke up this morning I thought I'd go out and play with my ball. So I went outside and got my ball, by the way I am a dog and I am called Zac and I am a West Highland terrier.

When I was playing with my ball I saw something in the sky, it looked like a bird but it wasn't, it was a plane. I tried and tried to jump up high to catch the plane but I couldn't, but I love catching planes. I wanted to go inside, so I went in. I was hungry, so I got some ham out of the cupboard.

When I had eaten all of my food I was scratching on the door again to go out, and I was let out. I didn't know what to do so I ran in the soil and it was lovely. I did that, then chased after the birds and went in for a sleep. That is the day of the life of Zac.

Sally Young (10)
All Saints RC Primary School

THE LAST DAY IN THE LIFE OF A SLUG

I thought, it had been raining. The ground was all dry where I was so I squeezed out from under the car onto the lovely wet pavement.

I rolled around on the wet ground. Suddenly, I noticed that the front door was open, snack time I thought as I slowly made my way up to the door.

I squeezed under the bright blue carpet and headed towards the side so that I wouldn't get squashed. As I slid along under the carpet, I saw a faint figure, it was a person coming towards me.

I think that whoever it was, noticed me through the thin carpet, because I heard a scream. I tried to hurry up to get out from under the carpet.

Slowly but surely, I made it to the kitchen, now all I had to do, was get onto the counter.

I went as fast as I could, sliding across the patterned kitchen floor.

About twenty minutes later I reached the cabinet, I tried to climb up the side of the cupboard. When I got halfway up, I started to slip. I couldn't be bothered to try to climb up again. When I landed I wriggled round to the front door and after about half an hour I made it. I crawled along when suddenly I saw someone enter the room, they hurried over to the high cupboard and pulled out, no salt, soon it was raining salt!

No!

Natasha Blore (10)
All Saints RC Primary School

A Day In The Life Of An Ant

I was awoken rudely this summer's day morning by my best friend's brother. I marched out of my lovely cosy bed, and out the door. Then I noticed him and my little brother were having their little leaf fights. I walked right up to them and told them to be quiet. But as usual, as soon as I went inside they started screaming their heads off again.

Then I set off to get some juicy leaves to keep them quiet. Also, we were going to have them for our breakfast. I collected the juiciest leaves ever. But on the way back a massive giant nearly ended my life. This is what happened. I had just finished picking the juicy, scrumptious leaves when I turned around and this giant's foot nearly killed me. I ran away as fast as I could. I dropped a few leaves but can you believe when I got back, they were resting and they were being quiet. So I thought I'd risked my life for nothing. As soon as they saw me with the leaves they darted up and jumped on me and ate all the leaves. Then I said, 'Guess what, that happened to me too.'

All of a sudden my best friend's brother got squashed by a foot!

Ben Carlton (10)
All Saints RC Primary School

A Day In A Life Of An Elephant

This morning I woke up, it was terribly hot and irritating, flies were buzzing round my ears. Then I noticed something green, but it had wheels. Suddenly a tiny man from inside it popped up and stopped when he spotted me. Then I really had to go. Jane, the chief of the herd galloped to me, my baby Ruth was stuck in the sticky mud! Luckily, Robert the oldest, moved her no problem. Thank goodness!

I was walking with my friendly herd to the sparkling oasis. On the way an extremely rude buffalo called me an 'ugly trunk' so I chased him off.

How refreshing! I bathed for a long time in the cooling water.

The leader of the herd is an old female sometimes called a matriarch. On this glorious day she decided to call a meeting. Jane looked immensely stern, she said in a frightened whisper, 'There is a fire. I don't want you to run, I want you all to help put it out.'

I stared at this mad lady but still obeyed.

The whole herd was toing and froing from the water hole. After what seemed like hours the fire was out. The sandy ground was charred but no one was hurt.

It has been an exciting day and I've learnt a number of things.

Kate Hulse (10)
All Saints RC Primary School

A DAY IN THE LIFE OF MY CAT

I woke up this morning and went to my dish to see if my owner Stacie had put my breakfast out.

No! She's late again. She woke up and when she picked me up I bit her. She knew that I wanted some food.

When I had finished my breakfast, I went out for a play and I was playing with the cat from next door and I was chasing a bird.

At 1 o'clock I went in to have some food and I went to sleep for thirty minutes. When my owner Stacie came home, she gave me a kiss and she hugged me.

At 6 o'clock it was teatime and I had finished my bowl of food. 6.30pm I went out to play for another thirty minutes and when it was 7 o'clock I went in for another restful nap.

Stacie Kearns (10)
Ashurst Primary School

A Day In The Life Of Clover The Pony

'Clover! Time for breakfast.' I poked my head out.

Yum! My favourite, apples, carrots, beetroot and Dengie oats. I don't get apples very often, although I love them very much.

'Clover!'
That was Marie, my owner.
What day is it? Uh-oh, Monday, I'll eat quickly to get this over with.
'Canter!' I wish she would let me relax.
'Clover canter!' So I did and she fell off with an 'Ouch, Clover!' I halted.

Later she had me put out in the field where I met Vinnie.
'Hello Clover, what's wrong with you?'
'Oh Marie fell off in canter, she had Mrs Alburn put me out here. I hope she's all right . . .'
'Not to worry Clover, see that's her over there, in the playground, it's okay Clover, she always sulks.'
'Clover, come on!'
I plodded over.
'Neigh!' I was happy. Kate Alburn, Mrs Alburn's daughter, always had Beth with her.
'Look, I had a long journey here,' Beth was saying 'you know I actually own that stable in-between you, Clover and Vinnie.'

After that speech, I was taken in and groomed until I was beautiful and shiny.

'So, are you okay Marie?'
'Yes, Mrs Alburn, but I don't think Clover is though.'

I was over in a corner of the stable afraid she would hurt me for throwing her off.

'It's okay, look, here's your supper.'

'Well Clover, tough day? Vinnie and I were playing races in the field.'
I gobbled up my supper and fell asleep.

Rhiannon Melia (10)
Ashurst Primary School

A DAY IN THE LIFE OF LEANNE CLARKE

Leanne is my best friend and I would like to be her because she is funny, friendly and interesting.

I was woken up by Leanne's cat Sox. I looked at the time it was 8.00am on Monday morning and I walked into the pub kitchen. I was greeted by Leanne's nan, the manager 'What do you want for breakfast?' said Leanne's nan.

'Usual!' I said. I got ready after breakfast, in Leanne's clothes, they were strange.

I walked to school at 8.45am and when I got to school I went into the hall to help Katie with the overhead projector.

At break Katie and I did the 'Hear'Say' dance with Lisa, Mark and Sam and we did the same at dinnertime.

As the hours and minutes went by it was ready for home time, I said goodbye to Katie at 3.15pm.

When I got home Leanne's nan told me to get ready for the dance class, which was at 4.15pm in Knowsley.

We did a dance 'Micky'. It was good, we were doing all different movements using our arms and legs.

When I got in I watched television and played computer games, I went to bed at 10.00pm but I couldn't really sleep as I had things on my mind, but I eventually got to sleep.

I woke up at 7.30am and found that I was at home in my normal bed - back as Katie Morrison.

Katie Morrison (11)
Ashurst Primary School

A Day In The Life Of A Spider

It was a beautiful day and I was sitting in my web. I was saying to myself 'I'm cool, everybody is going to like me.'

I got out of my web and began to walk over to another spider 'H . . Hello there!'

'Get lost!' it replied.

She didn't like me, I went to a few more spiders and they didn't like me also. Then I suddenly saw a hole in the fence, I had not seen it before. So I decided to go through it. When I got to the other side, it was a whole new world. Cars, people everywhere. I just couldn't believe my eight eyes. I went over to a park, it had swings even monkey bars. This was the best day of my life.

When I got up to the swings, I climbed up the bar and made another web, then out from nowhere a small spider was at the side of me. It was a young spider so I decided to put it on my back to see if I could take it to its mother.

I searched everywhere but she was nowhere to be found. Suddenly I saw a mother spider running around and shouting. This was my lucky day, she came running up to me 'Oh, thank you, I thought I'd lost him forever,' she cried.

Then she gave me a fly to eat. I was excited, I hadn't had a fly for a few days, then I went home to my web.

Jonathan Burrows (11)
Ashurst Primary School

A DAY IN THE LIFE OF KATE MORRISON (MY FRIEND)

Kate Morrison is my best friend, I have known her for seven years and I would like to be Katie for a day because she is funny and she makes people laugh. I want to find out what Katie gets up to after school.

The day began when I was woken up by Katie's three dogs, Jack, Jess and Joe and it's a good job they did because Katie has to go to school early to do the computers. So Katie's mum made my breakfast and then drove me to school.

When I got there I had to go straight down to the hall to do the overhead projector with Leanne Clarke, her best friend. When Assembly was over, I went back to class.

At playtime Leanne and I did a dance by J-Lo it was called 'Play'. The hours went by and before I knew it, it was home time.

When I got home I ate Katie's tea and then I had to get changed into Katie's dance costume because she goes to her dance class at six o'clock. When I got there I had to pay £2.50, then we got into our positions. We did two dances called 'Raining Men' and 'Wasn't me!' I had a really good time.

When dance class was over Katie's mum picked me up at 7.30pm and I went upstairs to bed.

When I woke up the next morning I was back to being myself . . . Leanne Clarke.

Leanne Clarke (10)
Ashurst Primary School

A DAY IN THE LIFE OF STEVEY KING (A WRESTLER)

I am Stevey King, a professional wrestler.

My day started when I was just trying to get some sleep, when the phone rang. It was the booker of the Federation. He said that I have a match against Dwayne Jokestone. He said he would give me the script when I got there.

I arrived at the Arena at about 6.00am. As soon as I arrived I was greeted by the Commissioner, he gave me the script. It said I had to throw Dwayne through a very thin window. But before I could do that I had to arrange it with him. So I knocked on the door, he wasn't too pleased about it but we sorted it out in the end.

I then had to go to my locker room to get ready. I kept thinking that something was going to go wrong, but it wasn't real, but I still had the feeling that something was going to go wrong.

As the cameras went backstage I was ready and I jumped out and hit him with the chair and punched him once or twice, then I saw the fake blood on the window. I threw him and he went straight through. 'What if he was hurt!'

Darren Northey (11)
Ashurst Primary School

A DAY IN THE LIFE OF FLOPSY THE RABBIT

'Come on girls, there you go, fresh food and water.'
'Hmmm! I'm more thirsty than hungry, but that carrot looks too good for Miss Mopsy to get her hands on.'
'Mopsy you can come out because you don't dig.'

Doesn't dig? The only reason Rachael's mum thinks Mopsy doesn't dig is because she never sees her and Mopsy's grey, so dirt doesn't show up very much. I'm black and white and my feet are white, so you can spot dirt on them a mile away.

'Ha, ha! I'm outside and you're inside. No more wrestling and eating grass. I'll just sit under your favourite plant whilst I eat my carrot.'

I see Rachael's mum hasn't put the brick across. A couple of nudges and I'll be out of here in no time! This is really my lucky day, the kitchen door is open!

No she isn't here. Hopefully all the doors will be open and I'll find Rachael. Is that toast? Yum!

'Hi Flopsy!' I wonder if my mum and dad know Flopsy has escaped?

If I can just jump up on the chair high enough I could pinch some of her toast.

'Come back with my toast!'

The garage doors are open, I bet Mopsy hasn't spotted that.

'Flopsy, where are you going?'
'None of your business, I thought you were lying down in my favourite spot.'

'I changed my mind.'
'Bye!'
'Bye!'
'Flopsy you should be in your run, I'll just give you a tickle.'
'This is brilliant!'

Rachael Smeltzer (11)
Ashurst Primary School

A Day In The Life Of James Smith (A Soldier)

Hello! My name is James Smith and I am now in the Army. I have been sent for, to fight in World War 1. My list of things to do starts with milking the cow but I'll skip that and tell you about the Army meeting.

As I approached the meeting ground, I was quiet, to make sure no one heard me. Soon after going in and being told what to do, we set off to fight.

We arrived there but it was quiet, which meant the enemy were hiding. Suddenly they jumped out on us. Luckily we'd all had training when the war started, just in case. So the fight started, I was ducking and dodging otherwise I would have been decapitated. The fighting was scary and lots of people were dying.

Sadly, people who had been there longer than me were dying of trench foot and shell-shock.

Soon they retreated, I had survived the first round.

We waited a long time, it was quiet which meant that they were hiding again. Oh no!

As soon as it was dark, they came, but we were now fighting a different way now. The sergeant made us go into no man's land first, so that the opposition killed us first. Yes they had now gone into no man's land as well, thinking we were dead. I killed one. I'd never killed anyone before, I felt weird. So you must go now, because it's night.

Natalie Jennings (11)
Ashurst Primary School

A DAY IN THE LIFE OF A POLAR BEAR

When I was going to the North Pole I saw a polar bear with three cubs and a father. The father had a baby seal in its jaws but the baby cubs could not eat it because they were too weak to eat.

We shot their parents with a tranquilliser gun from the helicopter and took the cubs to a health centre in Manchester. When the cubs got there they had a load of food, such as big lumps of meat, which we forced down the cubs' throats with loads and loads of milk.

When we took them back to the freezing North Pole, their parents were not there. We couldn't find them anywhere, so we went back to the centre and their parents were there. A person at the centre said, 'We brought them back because they had been shot.'
I said, 'I shot them to get the cubs because they were dying.'

So we took them back to the North Pole and I went home and snuggled into bed with some lovely caramel biscuits and a cup of hot chocolate. When I fell asleep I had a dream that the parents died and we kept the cubs.

Ian Westwell (11)
Ashurst Primary School

A Day In The Life Of Britney Spears

I got out of bed, had a shower and put my clothes on and went to rehearsals for my big concert which is tonight.

I had been rehearsing all day until it was time to have a party because of my success of being a pop star. I had been partying for two hours but when I came back, I just sat down and listened to one of my CDs that came out not so long ago.

It was time for my big concert. It was time to put my singing into action, but before I went on I had to get into my costume which was a red leather catsuit.

I walked on stage in front of around five million people. When I actually got on stage and started singing, I felt this fantastic boost of energy come straight to me to give me confidence in myself, which would be a very good help to me, considering it was my first live concert in front of these people.

I started off with 'Oops I Did It Again', which was a number one hit with my good fans. I sang several more songs and then ended the night with the song, 'Don't Let Me Be The Last To Know'.

After the concert I got a bath and went to bed.

Stephen Hurle (11)
Ashurst Primary School

A Day In the Life Of Darty, The Blue Poison Arrow Frog

The calling of the macaw wakes me. I guess I'll go and find breakfast. My name is Darty, I'm a blue poison arrow frog, one of the most deadly in the world. When a predator tries to eat me, poisons are released from my skin and *poof*, I'm out of its mouth in no time.

Let's look for some grub. Ants are my poison source. If I want an adventure I go to visit my closest relative, Spot, the yellow spotted arrow frog. His house is right through the rainforest. Let's go see him.

What the . . . I knew it. I just knew it, something has tried to eat me. I'll have to get ready to be spat out again. Weee!

Onward, if we go straight on it's Spot's house, let's go.

'Sss . . .'
'Oh hello Scales.'
'Are you going to visit Ssspot?'
Let me introduce you to Scales, the Burmese python.
'Bye Scales.'
'Yesss, bye.'

Here we are at Spot's house, we must be careful here. Look there's Spot and the kids.
'How are you Spot?'
'OK.'
'Is it OK if I stay with you for a while?'
'Yes of course.'
When I stay here we both eat ants, *yum!* Before I go to sleep I look out for a midnight snack. I'd best go into the house before he gets mad, bye.

Neil Doyle-Jevins (11)
Ashurst Primary School

A Day In The Life Of Bingo The Whale

One morning, the whale went swimming in the water. He was called Bingo. Bingo was waiting for his breakfast. He always had fish, every morning at 10 o'clock. When he finished, he jumped through some rings, then he entertained some people - he put a show on for them.

Bingo lives in a theme park. He got his dinner in the afternoon, he had more fish. He got his things ready. He was to perform in ten minutes. He was practising balancing a ball on his nose.

It was time for the show. Lots of people lined up to watch. Bingo came out from the water. They all cheered for him, for his first trick the keeper threw some fish and Bingo had to catch it in his mouth. He caught it.
'Brilliant,' everyone shouted, 'well done Bingo!'
Then Bingo had to swim and jump through some hoops. He did very well. The next trick was to balance the ball on his nose like a sea lion. The next was to jump through some fire. That was his last trick.

Everybody went home and Bingo swam round in the water. The keeper was very pleased with Bingo. Bingo was exhausted, he went to sleep under the water and the keeper slept in the house.

Samantha Dixon (11)
Ashurst Primary School

A DAY IN THE LIFE OF MY CAT

My name is Whiskers but my friends call me Puss. I live with my family of three and sleep nearly all day long. My owner brushes me, fleas me, worms me and how could I forget, she feeds me. The thing I hate most about living in *their* house is that they have a daughter and every time she sees me she pesters the life out of me. But, overall it's not so bad.

In the morning I wake up and go and find the owners. After I've found them I moan and moan and moan until they finally come downstairs and feed me, just to shut me up. After I've had my breakfast I go outside and laze around in the sun. Usually, five days of the week the owners go out somewhere and leave me at home for about six hours, but at least I have the whole place to myself. Then I go out hunting for birds. After I've finished doing that, I come inside and sleep on the bed until the owners come back.

Finally the owners come back and I run downstairs to get a nice tickle on my tummy. When they get home I'm normally starving so the owners feed me which then keeps me going until the next morning. When they have fed me I sit in front of the fire and fall asleep. When it gets late the owners go to sleep and so do I. Then the next morning I do it all over again.

Rachael Walsh (10)
Crosby-On-Eden CE Primary School

A Day In The Life Of My Dad

My dad works as a police training officer. That is a very important and busy job, as highlighted on Tuesday 22nd May 2001. I followed my dad around for a day. I feel that overall he is a very busy man. This is shown by how much he has to rush around and see to lots of different people.

8:30am: Set off for a long, hard day's work, down to Penrith.

9:20am: Arrived at Penrith.

9:25am: A colleague asked Dad if he could come back to Penrith next week and work some more.

9:30am: Went to photocopy some sheets about manual handling. Stopped off at a few offices to talk to some people.

9:40am: Dad discussed when he could come back to Penrith to work.

9:50am: We went into 'Class 3' to load some work onto a computer, ready to print off.

10:00am: We went for the printed off work.

10:05am: We both went to see the personnel assistant; she is the person who helps other people find police-related jobs.

10:20am: Went to the canteen. Dad talked to some more people.

10:55am: Dad had a class. He taught ten people all about manual handling. He introduced himself then went round everyone, asking them if they have had any past experience. He then asked what could cause a back injury. What things could be lifted. Then he put a video on, about ways in which heavy and light objects could be carried and how to prevent back damage when lifting heavy items.

12:15pm: Return to Carlisle for lunch.

1:15pm: Arrive at Carlisle police station.

1:45pm: We went for lunch.

2:25pm: Dad had a meeting with two people who wanted to move from another police force to Cumbria. Dad had to tell them all the qualities and disadvantages.

3:40pm: Finished meeting. Went home and collected my little sister, Alex, from nursery.

So in one typical day it is shown how hard my dad has to work. At the end of the day I am very tired and I understand that a job is a big responsibility.

But *my* dad can handle that!

Leigh Forster (11)
Crosby-On-Eden CE Primary School

A DAY IN THE LIFE OF AN INDIAN ORPHAN

My name is Kalyana and I am an orphan - but don't feel sorry for me, for an orphan who lives in India I am extremely lucky. You see, last year, an English man named John Foster changed my life forever. It all started in my village . . .

It was an uncomfortably hot summer's day, in the middle of the dry season and as my small brother Elijah and I were begging in the dusty square, we heard a rumour, an exciting rumour, one that might affect our lives. We heard an English man, living in the next village, was trying to build a home for the orphans in the surrounding area. Immediately, Elijah was desperate to go and meet this kind man. So, the next day, along with some friends, we set off at sunrise on the twenty mile walk along the sandy desert track to the man's home.

It was a tiring walk and halfway we stopped at a lone well to drink. Then we carried on walking - and walking and walking. My throat felt so sore and dry, my stomach was rumbling - but that was normal and I could hear the rest of my group chattering happily away. I didn't feel like joining them - I was beginning to wonder why I had been persuaded into coming.

By the time we arrived at our destination, the sun was setting behind the village in a furnace of red and orange light. We were all tired and dispirited but never-the-less, we did not forget our mission.
'How do we find him Kalyana?' asked Elijah - echoing my thoughts.
'Yeah, you're the oldest Kalyana,' agreed Cam - my best friend's sister, 'find him.'
'It wasn't my idea to come,' I grumbled, 'although I do have an idea.'
'Tell us! Tell us!'
'OK, OK - right if you,' I pointed to Cam and Gemma, 'if you knock on those huts over there, we'll (Elijah and me) take the other ones.'

We began our hunt. After an hour of searching in vain, I heard a shout - 'Kalyana, Elijah,' came Gemma's voice, 'we've found him.'
'Coming,' I yelled. Now Elijah was hanging on my arm, bouncing about like a kangaroo - even I was feeling excited as we ran in the direction of the voices.

When we arrived at Cam and Gemma we found them deep in conversation with a middle-aged, balding, white man.

'Yes, I was planning to build a home for some of India's orphans, but'

'But, what?' shouted Elijah.

'I'm afraid that won't be possible anymore.'

'Not possible?' cried Cam, 'we need a home! Why can't we have one?'

'Yeah,' agreed Elijah, 'I bet *you* have one.'

'True, I have but, well, I don't have the funds to continue the project - or enough hands,' the man spoke dejectedly. I almost felt sorry for him. Almost.

'You mean to say,' I asked, 'that we have travelled all this way - twenty miles - for nothing, in the scorching hot sun?' I finished.

'I'm sorry,' said the man, 'by the way my name is John Foster.'

'Well we'd better head back,' Gemma said wearily, 'we've got a long journey ahead,' and with that she turned and we followed her into the cool Indian night.

'Wait,' cried Mr Foster, 'come back, you can spend the night in my hut and in the morning I'll give you money for a train - it's my way of saying sorry.'

Then he stood up and wordlessly we, a tired, disappointed group, trudged after him.

Next morning, refreshed from a good night's sleep and a bowl of porridge, we said goodbye and thanked Mr Foster and left for the train station. But this was not to be. After five minutes of silent walking I had an idea, an idea to save John Foster's project. Briskly I told the others of my brainwave and then we walked as quickly as we could back to our village. The train money was going to another cause. This time the journey was not so tiring and in what seemed like no time at all compared to our first journey, we had reached our village.

Quickly, we gathered up all the villagers and told them our idea.

'We heard of a man who was building a home for Indian orphans,' I explained, 'but when we got to see him in the next village, he said the project could not go ahead because he did not have enough money or volunteers so I, I mean we, thought that some of you could help him out.'

I carried on in a breathless rush, 'At least that would sort out the volunteer problem and we could all make some donations - those who have money.' As I finished I scanned the busy village square nervously and to my surprise, after a couple of seconds, everyone burst into applause.

'Well done,' Gemma whispered in my ear. 'I'll collect donations.'

'OK,' I whispered back.

'Donations here,' she called and was almost trampled in a stampede of eager donors.

'Volunteers over to Kalyana,' she continued.

'Thanks Gemma' I thought as I was almost knocked over in a rush as well - but I didn't really mind, I was glad everybody wanted to help John Foster and the orphans of their country.

'Right,' yelled Gemma, 'any more donations later, volunteers follow us,' and the happy crowd followed us as we walked once more along that dusty sand track I was getting to know so well.

The journey went smoothly and it was a considerably larger crowd who arrived at the door of John Foster's hut a couple of hours later. I heard him sigh and come to answer our knock. When he saw me he sighed and began, 'Look I'm sorry but . . .' Mr Foster never finished. He had seen the crowd behind us, which rippled on like the ocean into the distance.'

'We brought some volunteers,' I told him.

'And some donations,' added Gemma.

'To help with the house,' said Cam and Elijah in one voice - trying to be helpful.

'We are willing to start work as soon as you need us to,' said our village leader.

'Thank you all,' said Mr Foster, 'I'll give you a brief plan of what needs doing and then we can start work immediately.'

So, after Mr Foster's briefing, the willing volunteers - and us - set to work. After just a few short weeks, a beautiful house stood, along with a wonderful garden and John Foster's dream had come true. He had built a home for some of India's many orphaned children and I had a home - so did Elijah, Cam and Gemma.

I am now old enough to go to the city for a job, but I am going to stay and help John Foster. The orphanage is now a village in itself - complete with a farm and even a theatre. I am glad for John Foster as he changed my quality of life and gave me a chance for survival - something many orphans just don't get.

Jennifer Ruddick (10)
Crosby-On-Eden CE Primary School

A DAY IN THE LIFE OF A COIN

My day starts when I wake up to a very dark morning. Sometimes through the day, I see a little light brighten up the whole of my very busy home, but not much.

I haven't got many friends or a proper home, since I travel around the country, stopping at many banks, tills and purses on the way.

After I have had my breakfast (coin drops), I sometimes play my favourite game, tig. By the way my name is 20p. I am just slightly bigger than one of my best friends, 1p.

If I could, I would have a bath but I believe that the queen on me is beautiful without one. Although, when we get dropped and it rains, that is our bath-time. Those are the days when I enjoy life because I have light and most of all *fresh air.* This lasts for about half an hour and then a child sees me, picks me up and says, 'Wow, this is good luck.' Then I get dropped into a small, leather purse which is my home.

Towards dinnertime is when I am most likely to be used. I am usually having my midday nap when cries of despair awake me. There is a soft, giant, peachy-pink, spider-like figure and cries from my friends, who are now huddled together in the corners of their home. *Who is going to leave?*

Suddenly I find myself in a McDonald's till with all the rest of the 20ps. In no time at all, I then find myself in a furry and cosy new home. 'This is my new home now,' I think to myself.

Emma Routledge (10)
Crosby-On-Eden CE Primary School

A DAY IN THE LIFE OF MY CAT, SUKI

Hi, my name is Suki. Every day my owner, Lucy, wakes me up at 8:00 and holds me in her arms. She says the same thing every day, 'Hello you cutie pie, what have you been dreaming of today?' It gets ever so annoying. She opens my breakfast and puts it on the ground. Sometimes she teases me with it. I gobble it up as fast as I can. Today it was chicken flavour, my favourite.

I went out into the back garden through the cat-flap. I saw a bird, I crept up to it and pounced. I just missed it, I was very annoyed. I went and climbed over the fence and went into the front garden. I just rolled on the grass and licked myself for a while.

Next, I set off to the park that's just around the corner. I climbed up the tree and went to sleep for about an hour. After that I got down, it was 3:15. At this time I normally go and meet Lucy. I saw her coming down Flagwood Avenue, she was walking with Emma and Amy, her best friends. Amy loves cats, she's got one herself. She came up to me and picked me up. I love it when she does that, she is so nice to me!

After that we just played together until teatime, it was great. After tea, I went outside again and played with my friend Maisy. I came in at 9:00 and went to sleep in my cat basket.

Lucy Milner (11)
The Dale Primary School

A Day In The Life Of Shelly

'Mum I've won, I've won, I've won!'
'Won what?' said Mum.
'I get to spend a day with Jennifer Lopez,' said Shelly.

The girls will go shopping, then go out for lunch, then go round Jennifer's house, then on to the shopping mall. Jennifer gets to draw two thousand dollars in cash from the machine and they get a thousand each to spend. That's a lot of money!

Jennifer was very nice and they got on surprisingly well. For two hours they went in and out of shop after shop and in the end they had spent nearly all the two thousand dollars, so Jennifer suggested they go for lunch at Pret a Manger which was the most upmarket restaurant in Swashey Pike. Shelly said that she had never been there before because she had never been able to afford it, but she would love to go now.

When they had chosen and eaten from the fantastic menu, Jennifer asked Shelly if she had room for a dessert. Shelly chose an ice cream in an elaborate cone and Jennifer had a lemon meringue with cream. Jennifer paid the bill and the chauffeur driven car from *Mizz* magazine took them back to Jennifer's house.

Shelly was so excited when they arrived but also a bit nervous. Everything was fine, Shelly liked Jennifer's house and they had got on well together because Jennifer thought Shelly was polite and well mannered.

Next stop was the recording studio where Jennifer made all her records and videos. Jennifer showed her round and then as a treat, Shelly got to sit and watch as Jennifer filmed a video for her latest hit single, 'Play'.

When the day was over, Shelly told Jennifer that it had been the best day in her life ever and thanked her. Jennifer was very pleased and said that she had enjoyed the day too and that she would send Shelly tickets for her next concert and they could meet up again then. Tired but very, very happy, Shelly was driven home in the limousine, a great end to a fabulous day!

Kelly Marr (11)
The Dale Primary School

A DAY IN THE LIFE OF STEVEN GERRARD

I woke up at eight o'clock and got dressed. I ate my Shredded Wheat and went to training.

When I got there, Phil Thompson told us we were playing Manchester United at Old Trafford and if we won, we were in the Champions League.

The next day at training, the manager told us the starting line-up. It was:

Westerveld

Carragher   Henchoz   Hyppia   Babel

Murphy   McAllister   Me   Berger

Owen   Fowler

I was so pleased to be playing, but I wanted to make a big impact on the game.

On match day I was so nervous. I was playing against Roy Keane. When we were in the tunnel, I started to shake.

We started well, with good attacking and then I scored a whopping shot high to the goalkeeper's right.

Our luck got better and better, when Robbie Fowler put it away to seal the game. After the game I had a beer and went home.

Matthew Price (11)
The Dale Primary School

A DAY IN THE LIFE OF JACQUELINE WILSON

I am woken up by the ring of my alarm clock. I peer sleepily at its face. It is 8am. I wander down to the kitchen and have breakfast. Then I write some letters to readers, have lunch and read. Soon it is 5pm. I jump up and race upstairs. I change, ring for a taxi, then step back and look at myself. This is it, I tell myself. Tonight is the night.

By 7.45pm I'm there. I look up. Smarties Book Awards. I sigh. There is Tony Ross, Ian Whybrow, Michael Morpurgo, Edgar J Hyde, Terry Deary - so many other authors all hoping for the same thing - first place. I saw Anne Fine walk in. I followed suit.

I crossed my fingers, crossed my toes, squeezed my eyes shut and wished.
' . . . And the winner is . . . ' The crowd held their breath. '. . . The Suitcase Kid, by Jacqueline Wilson!'
I forced my wobbly legs up onto the stage and smiled nervously. I had won! A second later, I was there, collecting my award. I felt happy and very proud and wished that I could be up here next year collecting another prize.

Alice Robinson (10)
The Dale Primary School

A DAY IN THE LIFE OF ALAN TITCHMARSH

Beep, beep, went my alarm clock at six o'clock in the morning. This is because we were going to start filming a new series of Ground Force.
After I had finished waking up, I had my breakfast of eggs, bacon, fries, mushrooms and French snails. But then, there was some bad news from the cameraman. Tommy and Charlie had gone to collect the concrete mix and wouldn't be back until we had started filming. Oh no!
Just then, I looked at my watch. I was twenty-five minutes late! I jumped in the Ground Force truck and raced off to a place called Pontlyfrie in Wales.

When I arrived, the director came up to me and said, 'Why are you late?'
I replied, 'Because I got some bad news.'
Then he introduced me to the person who had asked us to come. His name was Rob and it was his mother's garden. He wanted it done for her eighty-first birthday.
As I walked into the garden, I realised what a tip it was. It had plants growing all over everything. Just then the director shouted, 'Take one, scene one.' We were off.

To start off with, we had to dig up the lawn, which took us from ten o'clock to twelve noon. Then Charlie and Tommy arrived. They had picked up the concrete mix and Will, the handy man, along the way.

We started to put the concrete down. As soon as we had finished, it started to rain. It rained for two hours, which meant all we could do was order the plants and the water feature.

It was four o'clock and the lady was coming back at nine o'clock at night. We had just five hours to complete the job. We started to pump out the water which had gathered during the rain and while that was going on we started to put in the plants. Our main plant was a pink one. While Charlie and I were doing that, Tommy installed the water feature, which was a fountain coming out of a stone dog's mouth. By then it was nine o'clock and we very quickly tidied up the garden and waited . . .
Would the lady like it?

The eighty-one-year-old lady arrived back on time. She was absolutely amazed at what had happened to her garden. However, we were glad that she thought it was beautiful. We all finished our day watching the sunset while we each sipped a glass of champagne. We felt very tired after that long day's work.

Graham Cruickshank (10)
The Dale Primary School

A DAY IN THE LIFE OF A DOLPHIN

At 12am I say good morning to my best friends. At 1am I eat fish for breakfast and have a really good time with my family.

I see some people in a boat and swim to the crystal top to make the people jump. I do a big dive out of the water! I have the best time in the crystal water every lovely day.

I dive back into the water and splash around with my friends. I have great fun. My mum calls me and tells me to go and find my baby sisters, Charlotte and Suzanna. I look everywhere for them, but they are just nowhere to be seen. Then I hear them playing in the Sea Park, so I join in.

I take them home at about 7pm and Mum is quite angry, but Dad doesn't mind!

We eat fish for tea and watch television together.

Jenny Goodall (11)
The Dale Primary School

A Day In The Life Of Bart Simpson

Bart gets out of bed, looking for trouble.
He goes downstairs and teases Lisa and Maggie. Then he gets ready. He puts on an orange top and some blue shorts.
He walks to school with Millhouse. When he gets there, he takes his bag off and then sits down. But he doesn't get to work. He messes around with Millhouse and then he gets a detention.
After the detention, he goes home and watches the 'Itchy and Scratchy Show'. Then he tries to take some of Homer's beer.
After that he goes to bed.

Adam Darby (11)
The Dale Primary School

A Day In The Life Of Michael Owen

We arrived in Dortmund, Germany, on Tuesday 15th May and went to discuss the starting line-up. It was Westerveld, Hyppia, Henchoz, Babel, Carragher, Gerrard, McAllister, Hamann, Smicer, Owen, Heskey. We were then told to get some sleep for the next day's game.

The next day I woke up quite early and had a chocolate bar. Then I went down to the pitch to train. About five minutes after, the boys came down and we were all training. I passed to Gerrard and he smacked it in the back of the net.

That night in the tunnel, my legs were shaking. I was really nervous.

We shook hands, then ran out and got started.

We started really well. We scored in the fourth minute with Babbel, from McAllister's corner. Then it calmed down a bit, but in the eighteenth minute we scored. I had laid Gerrard on and he had scored, but in the 23rd minute they pulled it back to 2-1 to us. In the 34th minute I was brought down by their goalie, so McAllister put it in to make it 3-1 and that's how it ended at half-time.

In the first five minutes of the second half they scored two goals to make it 3-3. In the 66th minute Heskey came off for Fowler. He scored in the 70th minute. Then I came off for Berger. They scored in the 87th minute to make it 4-4 and take it to extra time.

In that time we won a free kick which McAllister took. It came off their defender's head and they collected the cup.

David Whelan (10)
The Dale Primary School

A DAY IN THE LIFE OF A GUINEA PIG

9.00am - Wake up in the morning, nice and comfortable in my warm bed. I get disturbed by humans trying to put me in a cold run. I try to escape, get stuck in the doorway between the bedroom and the food bit. The human grabs me. I fail again.

1.30pm - Yum! Here comes dinner. Oh no, it's dandelion leaves again! Right, that's it, I'm going on strike. I'm going to sit in the box.
A few hours later I go out to graze. Yuk! Muddy grass! Oh, what's this? Vet's day! Oh no! Last time I had an injection, the vet did it in the wrong place and then I had to have it again the same day! Oh no, it's my memory - it's vet's day tomorrow! Phew!

8.45pm - Ouch! I'm getting bitten by midges. Ah, here comes a human to put me away in my hutch. I love playing my game with them. It's good fun being black. Every time they try to grab me, I dart to another corner. You really must try it. That's if you are black like me, Sooty, because if you are, they can't see you. Oh drat! The human caught me. Oh yes! It's carrots and cucumber, not dandelions! Lucky me. Better eat it before the others come, I would never get it then.

9.10pm - Yum! I enjoyed that. Now I can go to bed. Mum and sisters are still eating. I'm going to sleep . . . zzzzz.

April Freeman (10)
The Dale Primary School

A Day In The Life Of My Hamster

Every day I wake up in my little house. I climb up the ladders and eat my food and take a little spin in my wheel. I wait for my owner to come down. She opens the cage and picks me up.

I love being stroked, but not too hard, and crawling up people's jumpers. After my owner left, I climbed to the top of the cage and found she had left the lid off. I climbed out of the cage and onto the floor. I crawled all around the room. Finally, a cupboard appeared and I climbed in. It was heaven. There was lots of food scattered in the cupboard, but I needed a drink.

At around 4pm I heard shuffling. It was my owner, she'd found me. She was hugging me and kissing me on the nose. She gave me lots of hamster chocolate drops. She put me back in the cage and gave me lots of lettuce, cucumber and tomatoes. Soon I drifted off to sleep. My owner came in and gave me a cuddle, then said goodnight.

I had a quick spin in my wheel, had a drink and went to bed in my little house at midnight.

Hayley Gee (11)
The Dale Primary School

A DAY IN THE LIFE OF FRED FLINTSTONE

In the morning Fred wakes up and has his Dino-Crispies. He goes out in his running car to the mine where he works. He uses the dinosaur crane. The boss pulls the poor bird's tail which makes a horn noise. Fred slides down the dinosaur's tail to the catchy theme tune. He jumps back into his running car and goes home.

His pet dinosaur, Dino, comes and jumps on him. In the evening he goes to the drive-in movie and he buys an overweight rib, which tips his car sideways. He watches the movie, 'The T-Rex Returns'.

Afterwards, Fred and Barney go bowling. Barney gets a strike, Fred does not. Later, they go to the burger bar and have a double cheese brontosaurus burger.

When he gets home, Fred has a glass of beer in a hollow mammoth horn and Wilma has some wine. They watch the telly, then they watch the stars and go to bed.

Daniel Faram (11)
The Dale Primary School

A DAY IN THE LIFE OF A DRESSAGE HORSE

6.00am - I wake up, have my breakfast and get Rio's dressage clothes ready. My mum drives me to the farm.

Laura tells me to get Rio before we go to the show and I take her for a ride. After that I give her some food and drink and then I groom her.

Later, my mum drives me to the show with Rio in a horse box.

When we get there, I put Rio's saddle on. It is jumping first and that is easy. After that I groom Rio and my mum helps me put on the dressage. The showman shouts 'That horse has a good temperament and is a good breed.'

I take Rio for a drink and some food. After dressage it's the races. I put on Rio's normal saddle and stirrups, get on and the judge shouts 'Go!'

We are off. Rio and me are in the middle, but we come to the front. We go into a gallop. I shout, 'We have won!'

We come first in all the events - dressage, jumping and the races.

B 1st Riding School are very proud of me. The boss's wife says I can look after Rio and I am entered in another show.

Nichola Carrington (10)
The Dale Primary School

A DAY IN THE LIFE OF ME

I woke up at 8.30am and went downstairs. I had Weetabix with hot milk - my favourite. Then I watched TV until 9.30am.
At 9.35am I went upstairs and got dressed into my riding jodhpurs, T-shirt and jumper. I went back downstairs and put my riding hat and boots on.
'Nikki, it's time to go. Claire will be waiting,' said Mum.
'Righty ho,' I muttered.
I jumped into the car and we set off to go horse riding in Hyde.
'Have you got everything? Toothbrush, pyjamas and slippers?' said Mum.
'Yes, don't worry. I'll see you tomorrow,' I laughed. I gave my mum a kiss and she drove off.

Claire, Rebbecah and Rachel were waiting at the gate. We climbed on the horses and set off down the track.
'Claire, are we going down to Green Hill meadow?' I asked.
'Yes, but we have to cross the road,' replied Claire.
Claire bent down to press the pedestrian crossing button, but she fell off. We had to get an ambulance to take her to the hospital. When we arrived, we found out that she had broken both her arm and leg.

Me and Rebbecah went back to the farm and cleaned the stables and horses. My jodhpurs were covered in hairs from Solo's mane. After that we went to the farm shop and helped scan the eggs and then we wrapped some bacon up.

At 6pm we had tea and then we had to go back to help Andy with the vegetable packing.
At 9pm we went to the farm and then went to bed, tired from another long day.

Nikki Worswick (11)
The Dale Primary School

A DAY IN THE LIFE OF SAMANTHA MUMBA

I woke up at 7am. I had to be up early as I had a photo shoot outside the London Eye. I'm going to be modelling for the front cover of Hello magazine. I'm really excited. After that I had to go and record my first ever single. It's called 'Body to Body'. It was proving to be a hectic day.

I arrived at the London Eye at 7.30am. I had to have all my make-up done and it didn't help that it was absolutely boiling. I was modelling with Britney Spears.

After that I went to the Polydor Record studios where I had to record my single. It was a really busy day but I think my record will probably go far.

Tomorrow I am having my music video filmed and the front cover of my single filmed in America. I can't wait! I've got to go and pack all my stuff ready for tomorrow.

It's been a really busy day, but I'm just dying to see what America's like - all the big cities and skyscrapers. But now I'm going to see my family to say goodbye to them. I hardly ever get to see them and I really miss them.

I can't wait to see what tomorrow will bring.

Emma Wheeldon (10)
The Dale Primary School

A DAY IN THE LIFE OF DUDLEY THE PARROT

I woke up at 10am and started to squeak. A minute later Daddy came down and took the cover off the cage.

At 10.30am Daddy took me out of the cage and let me fly around while he took Mummy a cup of tea. I flew to the fruit bowl and took some grapes. Yum! Then I went right to the top of the cage and practised my speech. 'What ya doin'? What ya doin'?'

At 11am the phone rang and I picked it up. Mummy came again and put it down and put me back in my cage.

At 11.30am Grandma and Grandad came round and Mummy let me out of my cage to see Grandad. I started playing with his drawstring.

I had dinner at 1.10pm and then went back and pooed on Grandad. Ha, ha! I got put back in my cage.

I played with my peg until 4pm and then said goodbye to Grandma and Grandad.

At 9pm Mummy and Daddy kissed me goodnight and put the cover over the cage.

Goodnight Mummy and Daddy I said to myself.

Imogen Kelly (11)
The Dale Primary School

A Day In The Life Of A Pen

I was sitting quietly in a box minding my own business when suddenly a big, fat oval shape with sausage-like things on the end came and grabbed me. It carried me away and dropped me on this black conveyor belt. Next I was picked up by yet another oval with sausages on. It scanned me through a bleeping machine. Then I was thrown into a plastic bag. I had a bumpy ride to a car. Once or twice I dropped through a hole in the bottom of the bag, so now I'm black and blue, although my blood is, and always has been, black.

It was mayhem in the boot of the car. The bag rolled around and all the contents fell on top of me and I began to feel quite sick! The car stopped and all went quiet. Oh dear, the bag was picked up again. Then another oval with sausages on took things out of the bag. Oh no, it's coming for me! I've been picked up and carried out of a room. Ouch! I've been dropped roughly into a pen holder with other pens, some of them like me, some different.

Now I'm being picked up and someone is taking my lid off. I'm being brushed across a piece of paper. Oh no! All my blood is running out onto the paper. Phew! At last someone is putting my lid back on and placing me back in the cosy pen holder.

I'm tired now. Goodnight.

Thomas Woolley (9)
Darnhall Primary School

A DAY IN THE LIFE OF A WHEELIE BIN

I was waiting for the bin men on a warm summer morning, though a breeze was blowing. My crisp packets were everywhere.

I hope the bin men get here soon, I thought. I wish they would hurry up. I'm beginning to smell so badly that the other bins are holding their lids and edging away from me!

Just then, the bright green van came whizzing around the corner. *Whizz! Bang!* The clamp grabbed hold of me. *Help, they've got me!*

Finally it put me down. I'm left feeling so dizzy. Worse was to come. The next door neighbour's cat, Fluffy, arrived.

'Go away Fluffy.'

She starts to scratch at me. Stop! Oh my poor green skin! What's that I hear? Woof, woof! Thank God for that dog. I'm saved. I never thought I would be thankful for a scruffy mongrel. Maybe next time I'll let him have a few of my scraps.

Oh no, it's my owner! Not that dirty, smelly ashtray again. Yuk! The thought of it makes me cough. My lid flips up. *Smash!* In surprise she drops it. Oh no, now I'm going to get cut from the broken glass. Nobody cares about their bins these days. The life of a bin is horrible.

All day long I let them fill me up with their bits of old food. I get spicy sausages splashed up my sides, left-over chicken, and socks that they've been wearing for months. On top of everything else, now she's left me here on the end of the drive.

What's this van now? The bin men have already been. Where are they taking me? Another clamp grabs me. Yippee! I'm being cleaned with disinfectant. When they put me back on the drive, all the other bins look at me in astonishment. I'm like new, the shiniest bin on the street. The life of a bin is wonderful!

Jessica Bannister (10)
Darnhall Primary School

A Day In The Life Of A Kitten

Hi, I'm Sophie. I have three sisters and four brothers. I'm two weeks old. This is my story:

I was asleep in my basket, dreaming that we had all moved house when . . . *bang!*
They're all gone, they're all gone! All of my brothers and sisters. Why? I know, I'll go and look for them.
I scramble out of my basket and try to struggle up the rickety-rackety stairs. Nearly there. Oh, aah! I've fallen. Let's have another go! Nearly there. Yes, I'm at the top.
Oh, what's that big brown thing? I'll see if they are in there. I scramble up and in . . . help!
Umph, at least I've landed on something soft!
'Mum, is that you?' Oh, it's not. *Boom! Boom! Boom!* What's that? Aahh, I'm moving. *Bang!* I've stopped. Now I'm moving again. After a while I stop. Suddenly it's light and my owner is looking down at me.
'Oh Sophie, what are you doing there?'
She picks me up and there's my mum, brothers and sisters lying in a brand new basket.
My mum licks me all over. My owner looks down at me and says,
'It's lucky I came and picked up that washing basket!'

Katie Brittleton (10)
Darnhall Primary School

A DAY IN THE LIFE OF A SNAIL

Do you ever think about being a snail?
It's so boring, I'm locked in an old empty ice cream box, with holes in.
Shhh . . . here comes the boy who put me here.
I want to escape! He's just taken the top off.
'You're rubbish, you are! You're always in your shell.'
He's grabbed me. Ahhh . . . ! I'm flying out of the window. *Help!*

'Ha-ha, I thought you might want a ride. Your name's 'Speed' by the way!'

I think I'm going to cry. No I'm not! I'm strong. Yes I'm strong!
What's this I'm on? It's all bobbly and it's moving.
It's a piece of wood with wheels on.
Oh no! Ahhh . . . ! Slow down! Slow down!
'Err!' A voice suddenly screamed. 'It's . . . it's a snail!'
Ahh! Something just pushed me right off that piece of wood.
My shell hurts.

Oh no! What's this? It's big and it's got sharp claws and big white
sharp spikes in its mouth. Ahh! It's going to get me! Bang! Bang!
Aww! Don't hurt me! *That hurt!*

Miaow!
That stupid beast just hit me really hard, whatever it was.
I think I'll go for a long slither down this hill.
Ohh! Ahh! It's a monster with wings.
It's coming down to me! *I'm going to die! I'm going to die! Ahh!*

Kimberley Stockton (10)
Darnhall Primary School

A Day In The Life Of Me, The Sock

Here I am being brought up by a smelly foot.
I don't know how it gets so sweaty, and of course he makes me smell as well. People sniff me, wash me and I get so dizzy, I just can't stand up.

I try to get my friend the trainer to tread in puddles so that I can have a wash without going round and round and round, but it doesn't work, I just get dirtier.

After that the foot's owner puts me on a quick wash; it's like he doesn't know that I detest the washing machine. So I have to live with him as he is for the rest of my life. I don't know how I'm going to do it. I'll take each day as it comes, but I just can't stop thinking about it.

The old days were great, sitting in that shop with all my mates, except for the women's underwear shelf!

Ouch! What was that? Oh no! I've got a hole . . . I've got a hole!
How, why? I want to know who did this? I want to know!

Ouch, ouch, ouch, that hurts! A long thin shiny sharp steel thing is piercing my woollen skin. What are they trying to do?
Oh my hole's getting smaller and smaller and even smaller.
It's disappeared! Good, now I'm back on his smelly old foot.

Holly Morton (10)
Darnhall Primary School

A DAY IN THE LIFE OF THIS WRITING

Well here I am being brought to existence by some grubby unsharpened pencel. Oops! Spelling mistake! Just wait until I change it. I'll bet that the boy who is writing me is dying to make a few more.

I think I look untidy. Is he deliberately taking advantige of me? Oh no, not another spelling mistake! I'm not enjoying this. I don't know how to correct myself because I'm not in control. Maybe I should see a teacher. She'll be able to put me right.

Ooops! Here I am talking about my private life on a piece of paper which the whole world might see. Maybe I should change the subject!

Mmm, what is there to talk a . . . Oh my goodness, I've just had a brainstorm! It's a bit small, but it'll do.

Now don't all pieces of writing have a title?
Ah, there it is *A Day In The Life Of This Writing . . . This writing!*

Since when has my name been *This writing?* I am outraged and . . . huh I didn't realise I was growing. Come to think about it, I'm *huge!* I've stretched so much I've split in two! Oh wait, I can't do that. I'm just a bunch of words. Well, my paper has split! *H E L P!* My paper has *ripped!* Oh I forgot nobody can hear me. I'm silent *words.* Why should anybody listen to pencil marks? What's the point in life if you're just going to fade . . .

Oliver Benjamin (10)
Darnhall Primary School

A Day In The Life Of A Tree

'Woof! Woof!'
'Miaow!'
'Can't I get any peace around here?'

Oh, it's only the morning and they're at it already, scratching my trunk and rustling my leaves. One day, one of them is going to get stuck up here.

At least it's not raining like yesterday, that must be why there're so many humans around. From up here they look tiny, like toys. They must see me as a giant as I'm as huge as a house.

Wait a minute, what's that one doing down there? It's not . . . it is! It's taking all that lovely grass away. I love that grass, everyday I watch it grow and see soft pink blossom from my long spindly branches float down onto it. It's making such a racket about it too.

'Ouch!'

Phew, it's only the woodpecker coming for lunch.

Lunch, I must have slept longer than I thought. It's starting to get quite chilly. Please say we're not going to have one of those flashing rumbling storms.

'Honk! Honk!'
What on earth . . . ? Humans with bright red noses, and what are they smiling about? Music! They sure want to be noticed.

'I'm trying to have a nap up here!'
Ow, what was that?
'Hey stop!'

A human is climbing me, who does it think it is?
Ow, ow, ow!
'Got it!' it cries.

Got it, you've got it alright, got hold of my branch. It's holding one of those bouncy, get stuck up tree things - again.

Now for my (yawn) nap.

Robyn Walker (10)
Darnhall Primary School

A Day In The Life Of A Piece Of Bread

It doesn't seem very long ago that I was sitting in a bag in a supermarket minding my own business, when I heard a rustling sound. We, that's of course, my friends and I, were tossed about all over the place. (It took us a while to figure out what had happened!) We had been taken out of the supermarket and put into the boot of a car. It was a very bumpy ride!

My friends and I were carried out of the car and put into a dark storage place. A big hand came and took one of my mates and another, then another! It was coming again, it was coming for me this time. *Ahhh help!* I was put sideways into a dark piece of metal, it had small red and orange lights inside. Ouch that's hot! The same hand came again and took me out of the hot object. Some yellow smooth stuff was spread on me, which soon began to melt. I felt my body oozing. I was cut into two. Both sides of me were taken off the wide, round, slippery piece of china and put into a large red hole with hard, sharp, white spikes, which crunched me up and I went skidding down a narrow tunnel.

I don't know where I am now, all I know is that I'm in a very dark place. I don't know how to get out and I'm scared of what is going to happen next.

Bethany Clewes (10)
Darnhall Primary School

A Day In The Life Of A Farmer

I woke up on a cold icy morning, the wind was blowing. I thought to myself, I'd better get on with my work.

First I walked unsteadily up to the milking shed, battling against the wind to milk the black and white spotted cows.

Once the teats were on I remembered that Bessie the horse was foaling today! Quickly I ran to the battered stable where she was kept. Bessie had a foal lying on the straw, whilst she herself was galloping around with another foal's leg sticking out.

Oh no! She's distressed! I calmed her down and pulled the foal's leg out. I knew without looking closely that the foal was dead. Poor Bessie, she understood what had happened and I left her for a while.

Then I saw a man strolling around. When he saw me he came over. Before he could say anything I asked him 'Why are you strolling around my farm?'

The man boomed 'How much is this farm on sale for? I'm interested in buying it.'
I looked at him and said 'This farm isn't for sale.'
'Are you sure?' He said.
'The farm isn't for sale!' I told him again.
'Final . . .'
'*The farm is not for sale!*' I repeated.

The man then walked sulkily back to his car, and before he drove away I shouted 'The farm down the road *is* for sale!'

It was nightfall and I climbed into bed, I thought to myself, today was a *very* tiring day, I hope tomorrow is better.

Amanda Snelling (10)
Darnhall Primary School

WHAT AM I?

As I got up from the floor I ran across the kitchen floor skidding to land on my tiny tail. I barked like a wolf to go outside.

I was surrounded by grass, twice the size of me. I ran like lightning around the garden and spotted a kitten. I ran to chase it, but it got away.

As I stared into space on my back, wagging my tail from side to side, my mum walked in with her four legs shaking.

Mum and I started eating our breakfast out of our shiny bowls. As we finished, Mum started to lick my fur to clean me. My mum just lies on the floor and sleeps (she's boring) but she does have 'off' days and races around the house.

I often think I am the owner of the house and break a lot of things in the house like plates and vases.

My favourite foods are trainers and clothes. My hobbies are running around the house and breaking expensive things. I am not able to sleep well at night, so I run around like a mad thing on the loose.

Liam Graham (10)
Forest Park School

WHO AM I?

I lay in my wet damp smelly bed dying for the loo. I let out a bark, but all I heard was 'Shut up!' I felt so so alone.

I trotted up to the door, I put my head under the little gap at the bottom of the door and saw my owners eating their supper. I felt so sad, cold and hungry.

I scratched at the old rusty door, suddenly someone came in and belted me right across the face, a tear ran down my itchy unclean fur.

My skin hurt so much because of all the fleas on my skin, someone flung me outside, I couldn't move, I was so ill, hungry and cold.

I wished I was with my other owners, the ones who loved and cared about me, but they passed away and now I am stuck with these owners.

I fell asleep and when I woke up I was in a clean soft bed, my fur was clean and neat and I had no fleas.

Now I am waiting for a new owner with the RSPCA. Can you guess who I am?

I'm an unwanted dog.

Emily Sutcliffe (11)
Forest Park School

THE SECRET VISITOR

My short ginger hair brushes the green leaves as I sneak out of my new home towards the now deserted picnic cloth.

I stop, I crouch low, ears pricked ready to run back to my den if need be. Then I hear it again, closer this time. I can't work out what it is, it could be dangerous, so I run back to my den.

Yes that's my wife, I'm back in the den and she's here to welcome me home. She's sitting here waiting for me. Head alert, eyes loving, she's sitting with the black tip of her bushy ginger tail hidden behind her left leg. She stands up when I come in, she looks anxious. Her eyes asked the question for her 'Were you seen?' I shake my head and she sits down again.

At that moment our son comes bounding in and jumps on my back, only to jump back off and start attacking my ear. I spring away and leave him with a mouthful of hair. We carry on playing like this for a few minutes. When we finally stop he stands next to his mother and I look at them both 'What a great cub' I thought. 'What a great vixen!'

When the coast was clear I call to my family and we all have a feast at the picnic cloth. Being a fox is great!

Liz Gregory (11)
Forest Park School

WHAT AM I?

As I licked my lips and crouched down as low as possible, my hair twitched and my ears pricked up. The wild antelope in front of me was alert and wandering. I could feel the eagerness in my paws, the animal with tasty meat made my mouth dribble with saliva. My foot moved one step, but knocked over a stone. The antelope heard and ran. I ran as fast as I could after it on my own four legs, my small thin tail, with a busy brown end trailing after it. I paused, pounced and grabbed on to my prey's neck. My strong head and sharp teeth shook my prey to death.

I walked proudly back to the pride showing the other cubs and parents my prey. I walked to my father the King of the Jungle and showed him my catch. Proudly my father shared out the antelope between the hungry cubs and I set off for my next hunt.

By nightfall I had caught five antelopes which would hopefully be enough for the pride. When I went home the cubs and young ones were already resting. We laid down and started to eat. The other adults were waking the cubs.

I thought I had done well for the hunt for a young lioness.

Stephanie Kwan (11)
Forest Park School

WHAT AM I?

My name is Purrdey. I own a three storey cage with my bedroom on the top floor. My pet, Charlotte, plays with me every evening. She cleans out my cage every weekend. My toilet is on the second level of my house. When I am given something I don't like, I hate those awful carrots, I put them in my toilet to show I don't like them. Also on the second floor there is a bottle of water. On the first floor I have my gym. There are two exercise wheels and there is a train for me to run through and climb on. On every level there is a snack bar, I help myself regularly to the food.

My pet Charlotte is much bigger than me, she is a giant. She is very clever because she can walk on her hind legs. I cannot do that as I am a hamster, we are not built for that sort of thing. We are great climbers and our ears are good, we can hear the slightest noise. I am very curious and whenever Charlotte puts her hand in my cage, I sniff it before stepping on to it.

Charlotte Kew (10)
Forest Park School

WHAT AM I?

I walked through the classroom door to see the children sitting quietly at their desks, suddenly I saw what was coming to me, it was Michael the silliest boy in the class. He gave me a cheeky smile, as I looked at him I said, 'English grammar books out.' Luckily everybody did as they were told and I thought to myself, 'This is going to be a great day.' Suddenly I heard a silly comment! I know who had said it, so I said, 'Shut up with those silly comments.'

Finally it was first break. I went up to the staffroom for a well deserved cup of coffee.

Later it was another lesson which was unfortunate because it was oral work, so it gave Michael the chance to open his big mouth, when he did it was the worst experience of your life. We started the lesson. It was a lot better than I thought it was going to be, Michael never opened his mouth once, he was as quiet as a deserted house, it was a dream come true.

Later when there was five minutes left, they were dreadful. The noise was horrendous, it was like a bunch of football hooligans. Finally the lunchtime bell went, they raced outside like road runners and I went upstairs to a lovely cup of tea. I talked to all the teachers, it was the best break ever.

After, it was time to get back to lessons and look after them for over two and a quarter hours, but it was dreadful. An hour was like a day and I thought I wouldn't survive, but finally the bell went an I thought to myself, 'I am Mr Groves, the teacher survivor of kids.

Michael Carroll (11)
Forest Park School

WHAT AM I?

I stared at the golden sand, my eyes glowed. I have razor sharp canine teeth. I stared at the children, no one noticed me. I was locked in a rusty, mouldy cage. I smelt horrible. I hadn't had a bath for months and many days. The zoo keeper didn't even take care of me. Life for me is bad, dirty and horrid. I'm not golden yellow sand any more I am black coloured coal with grey patches. All these days I have been kept locked in.

I have always wished for a day when I would be washed and as shiny as I always wanted to be. I'm filthy and ragged. Only one bloodied piece of meat is given to me every day. They treat me with no respect. I could see golden sand in the desert, smooth sand.

It is Wednesday. Two bright children approached my rusty cage, and looked at me with their pleasant eyes. I knew that they would take good care of me.

'Lucy, Phil come here,' their mum whimpered.
Lucy and Phil, nice names, I thought to myself. I tried roaring pleasantly at the two children.

The night came and there I saw Lucy and Phil.
'We have both come to help you,' Phil said. They opened my cage door and gave me a warm soapy water bath, and some proper food to eat. I was a beautiful lioness again.

Lubaina Karimjee (11)
Forest Park School

FOOTBALL MANIA

As I just finished a ninety minute run around, kicking a ball in the back of the net we were through to the World Cup Final. We went out to celebrate our victory. As I walked down the cobble stones I tripped up over the kerb. I had sprained my ankle and I couldn't play in the final so I was resting it until the day of the final. I went and watched on the bench as both the teams marched out on to the pitch to begin the ninety minutes of sweat and shame.

After forty-five minutes we were neck and neck. Nil-nil. As they marched up out of the tunnel, another forty-five minutes drowning with sweat began. Then suddenly we were one-nil down against the French side. Two-nil, then in the last minute three-nil. All the players were crying as they walked up to collect their shiny medals. I limped up the stairs to get my medal, then I fell over, I hurt my foot really badly. I got my medal and went off to hospital. I went to sleep on a hard round bed. My back was hurting me. In the morning Rivaldo came and gave me some grapes.

Matthew Walsh (11)
Forest Park School

WHO AM I?

I crawled out of the cave in the sand. I was in the Sahara Desert. I swiftly crossed the sand and saw my prey. I crouched behind a clump of tumbleweed and hid myself in the sand. My eyes flicked from side to side as I watched the desert rat hop closer and closer towards me. He then jumped close enough for me to bite him, but he was too quick. I thought to myself, he got away this time but he won't next time. I carried on crawling, but with every movement I made I became hungrier and hungrier. I will be too weak to catch any prey when I see some, I thought. Then I saw him cleaning himself behind a tall cactus. I lowered my flat head and once again hid myself in the sand. I slithered forward and hid behind another tall cactus, edging closer and closer to the rat. He seemed to sense me and stiffened, I used this to my advantage. I sprang forward and before he knew what was happening I had eaten him whole. It was like a bucket of warm water had been poured over me, it was like a fire had been re-lit in my heart. I set off into the pink light of the setting sun to find more prey.

Elizabeth Walkden (10)
Forest Park School

MY PET, TINY

There I was, stuck in the Everett's house. It was a scorcher today and I couldn't take off my fur coat for it was stuck to my body. As I went into the kitchen to get a drink, a cat was lapping it all up. I could not believe it! That was my water, not hers. As she saw me, I started to run towards her at full-speed. She legged it under me and ran towards the stairs! as I skidded to a halt and tore down the hallway after her, I suddenly felt a great pain in my left shoulder. I realised that this was my arthritis playing up!

I had completely forgotten the cat as I lay down on my bed. Then I heard a noise like human footsteps. Someone must be going for a walk in the park. I stood up to see who it was (my arthritis was not hurting any more) and it was my friend, Marcus. He stopped, sniffed around and raised his back left leg towards my wall. I knew what he was going to do, so I shouted at him . . . and it worked as planned! He overbalanced and fell over. Then I saw it, the car was back, out came the Everett's. I jumped with joy as they came in! Mum gave me a biscuit. Nathan played with me and Dad gave me a hug. I am Tiny, the Everett family's dog.

Nathan Everett (11)
Forest Park School

WHO AM I?

It was two in the morning and I couldn't bear the thought of losing in the final as the new captain. Victoria tried to convince me to have positive thoughts but still it passed my mind.

Victoria fixed me breakfast but I couldn't eat. It was like an everlasting rash. It was time for training so I gave Victoria and Brooklyn a kiss. I said I'd call them once I got to Paris.

As I stepped out of Beckingham Palace and got into my Ferrari, I realised that the press would be following me, desperate to get a photo of my latest hairdo.

I walked into training knowing in thirty hours I'd be in Paris. We did a few moves before we departed.

At the airport I had time to call Victoria and Brooklyn. As the Club Concorde set off I began to think about them. Two hours later we arrived. It was only a day till the final. We stepped on to the pitch to feel the condition of the grass.

A day later Fergie, the boys and I were shaking. The bell rang and we walked on to the pitch. The fans were chanting whilst the opponents prayed. I introduced everyone and we began. They got a corner and headed it past Barthez. After half-time we came back with a curling free kick.

It went to penalties and if I scored we would win the game. With a deafening crash the ball went into the bottom corner. We had won!

George Mensah (11)
Forest Park School

A DAY IN THE LIFE OF A SPOON

The cutlery box opened. A skinny woman, Katharina, peered in and grasping me tightly, walked briskly into a large room painted vile shades of brown. A wooden table groaned under the weight of plates of party food, shining glasses, bottles of wine, mountains of presents dressed grandly in silk ribbons and cards with sickening poems and messages.

I lay still as the doorbell rang shrilly. A tall bespectacled man entered stroking his goatee thoughtfully. He spoke in a harsh voice and his clothes looked so silly, I couldn't help giggling. Next a beefy man waddled in.

'Get a move on Gerome, Desmond's doing a beautiful speech.'

Desmond was a round fat boy who shrieked for sweets. He announced in a high-pitched voice that it was his 11th birthday.

An hour later the food had all disappeared, leaving only the puddings. Desmond was in the middle of his sixth tantrum. Suddenly he smashed me on the table, my head nearly burst. He then plunged me into a scalding liquid and whizzed me round violently.
'He's just a little over-excited,' gibbered Katharina fondly.

Desmond grabbed me and dived into a chocolate cake. Wham! I was in a hot, smelly oven covered in chocolate. Two blood-red cannonballs loomed ahead covered in huge flakes of snow.

Tonsillitis!

There were black teeth and silver fillings everywhere. I almost fainted as I emerged from Desmond's mouth, only to find myself flung into a dishwasher next to some disgracefully dirty knives and forks.

No pride!

Kathryn Sharpe (9)
Hunter Hall School

A Day In The Life Of Minstrel And Squeak The Guinea Pigs

Early in the morning, as the gleaming yellow of the sun began to fill the sky, Minstrel and Squeak awoke with a rattle on their hutch door.

'Oh no, not the owners. Not at this time of day!' squeaked Squeak.

'Probably come to give us food again,' squeaked Minstrel dopily as he gave a massive yawn, which revealed his two long front teeth.

'And water,' added Squeak as he ran into a long tube in their hutch.

As the hutch door swung open a deep voice greeted them.

'Hello guineas!' said the deep voice.

'Aghhhh!' squeaked Minstrel as the scrambled over the sawdust and newspaper that covered the hutch's floor, as two large hands entered the hutch and scooped him up. Soon another voice but softer than the other deep voice said, 'Hello Squeaky, has he been calling you Tufty again?' The nickname Tufty referred to the tuft of hair issuing from his coat. After the deep voice had spoken these words another pair of hands picked up the tube with Squeak inside and carried it away.

When the tube finally touched the ground Squeak peered out of the end of the tube. He was in the middle of a cage made from wood with wire mesh netting around it, there was something moist under his feet, he smelt dew, grass and *lettuce!* Next to it munching away at a dandelion was Minstrel.

'This, *crunch,* is delicious, *crunch!*' he squeaked with excitement.

'Hey, give me that lettuce!' squeaked Squeak as he dived and began to munch away.

The day passed and by lunchtime the sun was blazing overhead making it very hot in the garden. Minstrel and Squeak were very glad of the shaded part of the cage. Then suddenly a chorus of miaowing came to their tiny ears. Three cats were walking towards them.

'Mmmm lunch!' one of them said.

'Scrumptious!' said another licking its lips.

'Chewy!' said the final cat his eyes gleaming. The three of them walked towards the cage, with a savage look in their eyes.

'It's the end for us!' squeaked Squeak.

'Not yet it isn't, they have to get to us first,' said Minstrel trying to sound calm. Then two booming voices filled the air as the two owners came into the garden charging at the cats. The cats fled, jumping over fences and squeezing through gaps in a desperate urge to escape. The two owners then returned to the house.

The day quickly fell into night and it was time for bed. The two owners were now emerging into the garden and from there began a struggle to catch us two guinea pigs. Finally with a quick movement from one of the owner's hands they caught Squeak. Now for Minstrel, they stood there for about ten minutes struggling to catch him, when one of the owners had an idea.

'We could lift up the run and then catch him.' This turned out to be a big mistake. Minstrel darted through the owners' legs and ran into the flowerbed. However, it was not long before they caught him. Then they tucked him into the hutch and went back into the house.

Squeak soon fell asleep but Minstrel stayed up and watched the moon, as it seemed to wink at him, but then he too fell asleep.

Andrew Corley (11)
Ladymount RC Primary School

A Day In The Life Of A Frog

Yaawwn, aahh, excuse me, I'm afraid that I'm a little sleepy. You see, I have just woken up from my hibernation period. I am now on my way to the pond, picking up my breakfast on the way. All frogs make their way back to the pond of their birth after hibernating, so that they can mate. It takes some frogs weeks and weeks to get back to their pond but luckily mine is not too far away. Ah, here it is now.

I have joined the rest of my fellow frogs, cleared my throat and have begun to sing. Us male frogs use our lovely vocal chords as a way of mating, we just sing our hearts out and wait for a girl.

I am swimming around on the back of my lady frog, Penelope. We shall swim like this for the next few hours, I don't mind how long it takes, I am thoroughly enjoying myself. We have now swum to the bottom and are laying our eggs. Penelope said that they will all be as handsome as I am. She actually said that I was handsome!

Our eggs are now laid and are lying at the bottom of the pool. In a few days time, they will float at the top and a few weeks after that, they will hatch into tadpoles and eventually turn into frogs. After three years, they will be fully grown frogs and will go through the same process as I have been through today.

Now, I must go to bed. I hope that you have enjoyed your day as much as I enjoyed mine. Goodnight!

Elizabeth Wastnedge (10)
Ladymount RC Primary School

A DAY IN THE LIFE OF TEDDY

Teddy was sitting, gazing out the window. He always wanted to fly like a bird or a ladybird or a beautiful butterfly. Teddy went outside, and tried to fly with a kite, flapping his arms up and down but nothing seemed to work so he decided to leave it and go inside. His sister asked him, 'What were you doing outside?'
'I was trying to fly,' Teddy said solemnly.
Then his sister went away and thought about how she could help Teddy fly. Teddy went up to his room and watched the birds fluttering around in the sky.

After about two hours his sister ran up the stairs like a zooming car and flew into his room. 'I know how you can fly!'
'How? How?' exclaimed Teddy jumping up and down in excitement.
'Helicopter!' she shouted.
'Where on earth would I find a helicopter?' asked Teddy.
'Well,' she said. 'Uncle Jim is coming down from Africa in a helicopter, when he gets here you could ask him really nicely if you could borrow it!'

So Teddy waited week after week until Uncle Jim arrived. When Uncle Jim came Teddy spotted him from the window and ran downstairs to greet him. A few minutes later he asked very politely if he could borrow the helicopter. Uncle Jim said yes but Teddy could not go alone. Uncle Jim had to go with Teddy because he was too small to go by himself. So when Uncle Jim had said hello to everyone they set off.

While they were in the helicopter, Teddy spotted a piece of rope. 'Uncle Jim can I use that rope to fly?'
'Come here then and I'll tie it round your waist.'
So Uncle Jim tied the rope round Teddy's waist and another one around his own and they jumped out of the helicopter together into the sky and flew like a bird, butterfly and little tiny ladybirds.

Teddy is Superman!

Emily Atherton (9)
Ladymount RC Primary School

A DAY IN THE LIFE OF MARIA

'Ready, steady, go!' The teacher's voice blared in the distance as year 5 sat on the benches waiting for their race. Maria sat alone at the edge of a bench.

Why did it have to be sports day? Why couldn't she have been ill today? And why did she have to be in a team with Angie . . . the worst girl in the class? she thought miserably.

On the other end of the bench Angie was fussed over by a group of girls. Her hair was shining in the sunshine and her eyelashes fluttered up and down. For the past week Maria had been laughed at and called names by Angie and her pals. Now she wished it was 3.30pm, home time. But it was only just after lunch and she still had to run her race.

Just as they were about to run the race Angie whispered to Maria. 'You had better win because if you don't there will be trouble and I mean it.' A short blast went and it was Maria's turn to line up. She stood up, tried to take a step, then found herself face down on the grass. She flushed red. Someone had tied her shoes together and it could only be one person, Angie!

Maria was fuming. In a flash she tied her shoes and rushed to the starting line. They were off! Maria ran like the wind. There was no one in front of her. She felt fantastic. On she ran, through the red ribbon and someone handed her a number 1 card. Wow!

Later as the teacher announced the Best Team Player Award, Angie felt so sure she was going to win that she stood up ready to receive the prize. The teacher looked oddly at Angie then boomed *Maria!* Now Angie was the one fuming. Tears of rage filled her eyes as Maria proudly stood up to receive her award.

Ciara Healy (9)
Ladymount RC Primary School

TRAPPED

I woke up in a cold sweat. I'd had the same dream for five nights running. I called for Mum but there was no reply. My mind was full of thoughts, could the dream have been a premonition? I couldn't settle so I went downstairs for a glass of water.

The kitchen back door was open and glass was shattered everywhere across the floor.
'Mum, Dad,' I yelled.
Suddenly someone jumped out from behind me.
'Where's the money kept?' he asked.
'I . . . I . . .' my mind went blank.
'I said where's the money kept? Answer me.'
'Mum,' I shouted.
I then felt a sharp stabbing pain in my side and I fell to the floor.

The next thing I knew was that I was in a cold, damp room, exactly like the one in the dream. I felt scared. Terrified almost. The door opened and closed. Could someone be in the room with me?

I got up clutching my side and walked towards the window. A faint light flickered through. I felt a hand rest on my shoulder. I gasped, was my dream starting to become reality?

I turned around to see a ghostly figure standing next to me. It took my hand and lead me out through the narrow gap next to the window. I was *free*! Or was I? I felt trapped in this nightmare. Only I knew what was to happen next . . .

Sophie Milosevic (10)
Ladymount RC Primary School

A DAY IN THE LIFE OF A TEA BAG

'Shut up Sam, they'll be here soon.'
Oh hello, I didn't see you there. It's so nice to see you again. If you don't remember, the last time we met was in the story The Night In The Life Of A Tea Bag. For some of you who have not met me before my name is Fred (the tea bag) and this is my friend Sam (the tea bag). I'm here to tell you about my experience when I got put in a cup of tea and most of my guts got sucked out (very exciting I can tell you that). It started off as a very boring day until it got to 9am. Because that's about the time Miss Griffiths has her tea. Us tea bags get up very early as you can see. She put her hand in to get a tea bag. I felt something grab me and I looked up and saw Miss Griffiths' hand round me. *Me, me,* out of all the tea bags in the tin, *me!* Little did I know what was ahead of me. She poured hot water in the cup and then put me in. The water was very hot. I heard my tummy rumble and saw my guts pour out and dissolve in the water. Then she threw me away. That's how I ended up here in the trash can. *Oh!* I've got to go. The banana peel has picked a fight with the apple core and since I'm the only sane thing in the bin, I've got to go and break it up. Ta-ta.

Rachael McAlister (10)
Ladymount RC Primary School

A DAY IN THE LIFE OF MY CAT, TIGER

Hi, my name is Tiger, well that is what my owners call me. Let me tell you a bit about myself. I am eight years old and my favourite food is fish.

My day starts when I wake up at about 7:45am. I wash myself and go into the warmth of the master's house and sit by the blower with the master's daughter, Kym. She takes up most of the blower, which is most annoying.

The thing I love most is playing with butterflies in the summer. It's breakfast time. *Yum!* My favourite, rabbit and chicken. But the only thing wrong is that Karen (Kym's mum) mixes it with biscuits and it spoils the taste of the rabbit and chicken. After breakfast I go out to mess around in the garden and try and catch butterflies till dinner. Then I have to have the same food again, the food I didn't eat at breakfast. Once I finish my dinner I go and have a sleep, a long one too.

I finally wake up at 4pm. My owner has some string out for me to play with. I run around and chase it for about an hour. Then I watch TV, well the owners' TV, then I go to bed.

Emily Old (10)
Low Furness CE Primary School

A Day In The Life Of A Snow Leopard

My life is all work and no play. All day I hunt for food and try to protect my precious cubs. But when I do finally get a break, I wash myself and my two remaining cubs. Poachers came and took my oldest four away. I wouldn't be surprised if some posh, snooty lady is showing them off from the inside of her gloves and shoes.

I also enjoy counting my spots and sunbathing in the sun. But there is one thing I do hate and that's where I have been today. You see, three men came today talking in their weird language. They had bait, it was a delicious chunk of red, juicy meat. The thought of not having to hunt lead me and my cubs into the cage. I fell asleep and when I woke up my cubs were crying for me. When I saw we were closed up with electric fencing I felt like crying myself, but no, I had to be brave. I told them that we would break out of this. So when they opened the door to feed us we ran and escaped. We are back in the forest now and I will never complain about my life again.

Helen Dyer (9)
Low Furness CE Primary School

A Day In The Life Of A Camel

I woke up on one of the hottest days of the year. It was so hot that I had to go for a drink.

In the oasis it was lovely and cold. When I wake up I don't usually need a drink till dinner time. I only need a drink at dinner time because I am exhausted from carrying people around on my back. At dinner time I eat grass and bathe in the sun. When I bathe in the sun I think of piles of gold. When people ride on my back I feel very important because I carry then around the desert. I went to the big old rock for a bit of peace. I sat there for about an hour and a half, watching lizards catching and eating flies for dinner, and insects climbing on the rock up above me. I went back. After dinner I start carrying people all around the Sahara desert. I went down to the oasis for another drink and stored about two litres of water for the journey home to my master. I have to go to the rocks to pick up my last passenger, he is my master's brother. Then it is off to bed for me. Goodnight everyone.

Dean Sewell & Christie Davies (10)
Low Furness CE Primary School

A DAY IN THE LIFE OF A SCHOOL RAT

Hi, my name is Kari and I am one year old. My favourite food is carrot (but I've only had it once in my life). Recently I had four babies called Oki, Tiger, Tigger and Rodney.

My day starts at 9am, when I wake up to feed my babies.
'Oh no my mistress is coming, hide quickly,' I called to my babies.
We all scattered and hid. Suddenly this giant hand reached in, it locked around me and lifted me way up off the ground. All of a sudden it dropped me 'Argh.'

I ran and ran and ran, not knowing where I was going. For three days and nights I ran over shelves and books, computers and lots of other strange things.

On the fourth morning I finally found my home and climbed into the safety of it. Later I found out that my mistress (Helen) had been sacked and that I could live a quiet, peaceful, happy life with my adorable babies.

After my babies had heard of my scary adventure, we all had a good feed, with all of my favourite food and a lovely cold water drink. I then settled back down to sleep with all of my babies. Bye for now. Goodnight.

Rachael Barton (10)
Low Furness CE Primary School

A Day In The Life Of Luxury

It was a Thursday morning and it was my birthday! I was really excited. I walked downstairs, everyone said happy birthday to me. I ended up with a big bag of presents. I got the Everton kit and a season ticket. Then I found out we were going to town for a day out. I begged my mum to go to Woolworths. So we went. I immediately saw a wrestling game for my PlayStation and bought it straight away. I also bought Harry Potter 2 and Pokémon cards. Then we went to some clothes shops to buy something for Hannah and Rhiann. Then we went to the museum but it was closed. So instead, we had to go shopping for clothes. It was really boring until I saw a mini radio set and bought it for £4.00. After that (finally) we went to Burger King for tea. I had a quarter-pounder meal with Sprite and I had an ice cream. Then we went home. Suddenly my mum pulled over at Edge Lane cinema. We were going to see Stuart Little. It was a really good, entertaining film. I really enjoyed it, I gave it ten out of ten. Then we went home. I had a go on my PlayStation game with was really good. So altogether I had a really nice birthday. You could say I had a day in the life of luxury.

Steven Jones (10)
Mackets Primary School

WHO I WOULD LIKE TO BE?

I would like to be Britney Spears, the popstar because she has got loads of talent plus she gets to meet loads and loads of famous people. I love her cool songs like 'Lucky' I remember her first song that she sang. It was called 'Hit Me Baby One More Time.' The clothes that she wears at her concerts are a bit mad but they are still cool. Her new song is called 'Don't Let Me Be The Last To Know'.

I think that is my favourite song up to now because it is very good.

Do you know what my dream would be? It's where Britney Spears would come to our school and sing some of her songs for us. Sister 2 Sister have already been to our school, it was very good, they sang about four of their songs for us. They are good singers but Britney Spears is much better. I think Britney Spears is better because she has been a singer for ages and Sister 2 Sister haven't been singers for as long as her.

So now you know who I would like to be but if I wish and wish every year or day to be Britney Spears, I doubt my wish would ever come true. Who would you like to be?

Lauren Jameson (10)
Mackets Primary School

A Day In The Life Of Geri Halliwell

'Come on Geri, get up' said her mum Jean.

Geri starts her day at 7am. She jumps in the shower, ready for her personal trainer, who arrives at 7.15am. She does her workout, which usually lasts an hour; she then goes for her breakfast, which is usually fresh fruit, and yoghurt.

After her workout and breakfast, she goes to her study to answer her mail. At 10am her chauffeur arrives to take her to the recording studio, where she is doing work on her new album. She stays there till 4pm. When her chauffeur picks her up and takes her back home. She just has time to take her dog for a walk before her hairdresser arrives, at 6pm.

She has a big celebrity party to go to tonight and she must look her best.

At 7.30pm her chauffeur arrives again to take her to the Brit Awards.

At the awards Geri wins an award for her new single, 'It's Raining Men!' The Awards finish at 11pm. She then goes to a party which is being thrown by her friend Emma Bunting. She leaves the party at about 2am, as she has an early start the next day. She is flying to America to appear on a talk show.

Louise Edwards (11)
Mackets Primary School

A DAY IN THE LIFE OF A POLICE WOMAN

I was really nervous as I drove along the street. I pulled up the car and this was where things really started to kick in, I felt really sick with nerves. I walked up to the police station, got into the uniform and went to see who I was working with and what I would be investigating today.

We were walking up and down town but suddenly PC Plod, my partner, stopped so I did. We saw two men just about to put black masks on. They got a brick and smashed the window. All the alarms went off. PC Plod counted to three, '1, 2, 3,' and we both grabbed his legs. We got them on the floor, tied their arms behind their backs and put hand cuffs on them.

We took them to the van and drove them back to the police station, when we got there, we handed them over to the custody officer to be interviewed. Then PC Plod and I went to get a cup of tea. Soon tea break was over and we were off on our rounds again. It wasn't long before we got a call on our radio about someone being shot! PC Plod said to me, 'There will never be an end to crime in this world!'

Jessica Campbell (11)
Mackets Primary School

A DAY IN THE LIFE OF MY PET JESS

Jess was lying on the floor when a giant aeroplane went past the garden like a rocket. Jess started to bark, then Michael took Jess for a walk, he fed her and they went to play in the park with her favourite ball. They walked along the sea wall and Michael got a dog treat for her. A cat ran past and Jess shot down the sea wall. Michael ran after her and said 'Come on Jess.' Jess got tangled up in her lead. A big lorry drove past and Jess barked again and shot down the sea wall. Then Jess went into a puddle and got soaking wet. There was worse still, a hundred cats ran towards them, it was show time! Jess shot down the road like a rocket and Michael ran after her like mad. It was like a scene for one hundred and one tabby cats.

The worst thing then happened, the cats turned back on themselves and Michael and Jess fled, it happened again and again and Jess got caught in her lead, she got herself free and shot down the road like a bullet.

Michael Clarke (8)
Marshside Primary School

A DAY IN THE LIFE OF JESS THE DOG

I woke up early that morning, just dying to play. I dived on my owner's bed and started licking her face with my rough tongue. Uggg! But she woke up all right. Yippee! She took me into the garden, I ran around frantically then she fed me. I gobbled my food and lapped up my water. I sat in my bed thinking what to do next. I went rooting through my bed and found a chewstick, yum, yum! I ate half the chewstick then buried it again. I love them you know. My owner has just come downstairs to make a cup of coffee, I think. She has got dressed, she's getting the lead, whoopee! I'm going for a walk, I'm going for a walk and you are not. Na, na, na, na, I am now on the field. I meet another dog, I thought we could be friends, we start out good but he wanted a fight so I gave it to him alright.

I won as usual. I think I'm the best dog in the world. Hang on I smell a cat. Charge! I just love the taste of fried cat, you should try it, it's delicious. We went home, my owner had a friend round for tea. It was sausage, mash potato and gravy. All I got was dog food. My owner's friend left. My owner washed the dishes while I curled up in my basket and fell fast asleep. What a busy day it had been.

Kayleigh Jones (8)
Marshside Primary School

A Day In The Life Of A Butterfly

I woke really early when I fluttered to the flowers to get my breakfast. While I was sucking my breakfast, I saw the horrible bees so I quickly finished my breakfast and flew off before the bee saw me. Eventually I flew back to my nest. When I got to my nest I decided to call the babies down for breakfast.

I took them to another part of the garden, when they had nearly finished, I saw the bee family in the sky so I quickly flew home with my babies. Then I thought that the bee family where following us. Gradually I put the babies to bed for their lunchtime nap, within moments I thought it was time I had a little nap as well because I was so tired. When I had had enough sleep, I woke up the babies and took them out for lunch at the Butterfly restaurant.

A few hours later, I decided to go down town to have a look at houses that were for sale in Reeds Rains. When I was in Reeds Rains, I saw the house I wanted. Meanwhile I was thinking if I should buy it or not. As time passed, I decided to buy it. When I got to my new home, I had a look round the house with my babies and I never saw the bees again.

Rachel Marshall (8)
Marshside Primary School

A Day In The Life Of The Grasshoppers And The Ants

One morning the grasshoppers were getting ready for an excellent adventure. The boss, Mr Hopper led them on the way. 'We are going to the corn!' said Hopper to the golden cornfield. Fatso his brother was not looking where he was and he fell in the river! 'Help!' shouted Fatso.
'If you still want to be in my gang, keep up with us!' said Hopper.
'What is that smell? I can smell ants!'
'What sort of ants?' yelled Hopper.
'Red ants, I absolutely hate red ants!'
'Let's shoot home quick, get all your kit on.'

They all marched back the special cornfield.
'Hop, two, three, four' shouted Hopper.

They were getting closer and closer and closer.
'Fatso if you fall in that river again, you're definitely out of the gang.'

'All get your potato guns out' said Hopper! 'All come here,' he continued.
'Why?'
'I've put antkiller in your guns,' shouted Hopper.
'One, two, three, squirt!' yelled Hopper. At last ten were dead.

Kelsie Buck (8)
Marshside Primary School

A DAY IN THE LIFE OF MY DOG

One morning I got up from my big comfy quilt and heard the postman posting the letters. I charged towards the window, jumped up onto the window shelf and I started to bark. Suddenly my mum came down from her bed and told me to be quiet. She poured me a drink of water. I ran straight towards it but then I knocked a plant and some type of dust fell on my nose. It made me sneeze. I started to feel funny, everything started to get bigger and bigger. I felt dizzy and I had a headache. I barked and barked but it was too quiet. No one heard me, it was dreadful, one of my worst nightmares, I've shrunk. I didn't know what to do.

I tried to climb the stairs, it was a task, I kept on slipping. I went outside and I met a bee on the table.
'What are you supposed to be?' asked the bee.
'I'm a dog but I've shrunk' I replied.
'I know someone who can help.'
'Who!'
So bee went to go and get wasp. Suddenly I saw them flying back, they landed and stood next to me. Wasp stung me and I started to grow bigger and bigger, it had worked! I am really happy.
'Thank you wasp.'

I felt really tired so I went in, had my dog food and curled up in my comfy basket.

Jade Evans (8)
Marshside Primary School

A Day In The Life Of An Ant

I just woke up, then I smelt some smoke. I went out to see, there shining before the sun was a magnifying glass, it was burning the anthill. As I was going to warn the others, they were already running out, next I got trampled on by the rushing ants.

A few minutes later, I got up but my leg was aching, my home was on fire, I got out and jumped onto the boy's shoelace. He set off to his house, he walked into the kitchen and kicked his shoes off with me on them. I climbed off into a dark hole. That would have to be my home for now.

A few hours later, I set off to find my friends to tell them about an apple I had found, they were under a leaf. I brought them to my house, I told them to help me move the big apple. It took us a long time to squeeze it into the small hole.

A couple of hours later, all the apple had gone and so were all the ants, they were all dead next to some white stuff. I walked up to it but then I saw some ant killer, that must have been the white stuff. I walked out in a sad mood, not looking to see if anyone was there. I was too late, I got stood on. I was dead!

Ryan Corteen (8)
Marshside Primary School

A Day In The Life Of Andy The Ant

I was crawling through the grass, I saw a lot of people in the town, the ant catcher is after me. He is the largest ant in the world! I got stuck on bubblegum on someone's shoe. I needed to get back to Antland, I managed to get off the shoe. I found myself in a river. I saw a frog, it's going to eat me. I jumped out of the river, I was running to Antland but a fly picked me up and I got stuck in its arms.

I landed in Antland. I saw the antcatcher blocking the tunnel with his evil army of ants, then my friend Alex came but his army took a rope and tied us up, he said,
'I want Antland forever!'
'Don't worry Professor Arnold will come!' Alex whispered quietly.

An hour past, the army were told to put posters up saying that that ant catcher wants to have Antland. Everyone knew what would happen to Antland. When Arnold found out about Antland, he knew we were in trouble. Eventually Arnold had came and said,
'I will throw shrinking powder over you!'
'I dare you!' the antcatcher cried.

He threw it at him and he was a tiny ant now, we are saved! And Antland is too!

Liam Smith (9)
Marshside Primary School

A DAY IN THE LIFE OF LEE FINEGAN

Lee ran around the park wanting to go on the tyre swing, he asked the girls to let him have a go but they said,
'No!' I scattered around with him and then we started to go home but the girl's cousins came and hurt his nose. I helped him get up from the ground and made sure he got home safely and then we went in his house. Later that day Lee had to go to his grandad's. He had a fantastic time, a squirrel ran up his arm, he made a friend called John. His older sister Michaela made a friend called Claire and Conor made a friend called Marc. He played and played till he could play no more. Soon they came home and Lee was asleep but he woke up when they parked. It was mid afternoon but Lee wasn't tired anymore so he played on his PlayStation. He played Mario, Spyro 2 and Croc 2, he completed them all in four hours and 57 mins, he was so pleased with himself, he had a feast upstairs, played with his brother and hugged his mum. After that he was exhausted and had a nap. He woke up at dinner time, just because of Conor. He went downstairs still tired and almost falling to the floor. After his dinner, he decided to have an early night in bed because he was really, really tired from all the things he had done this morning. He raced up the stairs and jumped into bed and went to sleep.

Andrew Smith (9)
Marshside Primary School

A DAY IN THE LIFE OF A MILLIPEDE

I was underground where my family was. My dad had gone out to look for food but my mum was asleep. My big brother Harry was digging holes while my sister was pretending to lie dead on the floor. I looked outside to see if I could see Dad coming home.

Five hours later my dad came home with enough food for all of us. After our delicious snack my mum told me to go to bed, my brother laughed at me but I ignored him. I tried to get to sleep but I couldn't because I kept thinking about that wonderful snack I had eaten. What if my dad had killed that snack I ate? That would be awful if anyone saw him, he would be picked on for the rest of his life.

Just then I heard a bang, what was it? I crept out of my dark and small room and I peeped into the living room, I saw Mum and Dad wrestling in front of my brother and sister. My sister cried but my brother kept sitting there moving his head wherever Mum and Dad went. My mum stopped and my dad stormed out from underground and made enormous big blobs of mud in the living room.

I went to bed when my mum stormed to bed, my sister was already asleep and my brother slept on the big comfy sofa.

Next morning I got up, so did my brother and sister and we all said 'Where's Mum?' She wasn't underground.

Sophie Slater (9)
Marshside Primary School

A Day In The Life Of A Ladybird

Lucy the ladybird was getting up and she went down all the stairs. She tried to get out of her door. Suddenly, it came flying back and smashed poor Lucy to death. As she got out it was burning hot that morning, she said to herself.

'Phew I am glad that I never damaged my wings because I would not have been able to fly.'

Lucy went to a post and guess what she saw, go on, have a guess, yes it was flowers and what happened when she flew down, well I will tell you now.

Well when Lucy went on the flower, she got trapped and she shouted,
'Help, help, I am trapped, please help!'
By lunchtime, Lucy's friend Alice went to Lucy's house but she was not there, Alice noticed her. Alice went to go and save her so she opened the mouth of the flower and saved her and this is what Lucy said to Alice.
'Oh thanks Alice, would you like to come to my house for saving my life?'
Alice suddenly replied,
'Erm . . . OK if you really want me to!'

Alice and Lucy were so excited about what's happening and then it was time for Alice to go home.

Within moments, a caterpillar came by and asked if he could play with her and this is what she said,
'Of course, you can play, what is your name?'
'My name is Kevin and my friend is Andrew.'

Soon Andrew arrived and it was late so they all had to go home, it was too late to play.

Chloe-Louise Pinch (9)
Marshside Primary School

A DAY IN THE LIFE OF A BUTTERFLY

It was a sunny morning, I looked out of the window, my mum and dad and sister were already up. I got dressed and ran outside. My mum and dad were sitting watching my sister Penny, she scared a butterfly and it flew away. Penny followed it, so did I, but suddenly it hit a little tree. I rushed to see if it was hurt but it wasn't.

'Phew' I said. My mum shouted,
'Penny come back,' I carefully picked it up, it was very delicate.

I carried it back to my house,
'What's that in your hand?' my dad questioned. At that moment I thought he must of been very curious. So I replied.
'It's the butterfly that flew off, it hit a tree so I've decided to look after it until it's fit!' A week had passed and it still wasn't fit, I was getting really worried.

After two more weeks, the wing had got better but still we kept it till it had fully recovered. When it was time to let it go, I released it by the river. It was really funny through because I could of sworn that I heard the butterfly speak. That night the butterfly returned and said,
'I just came to say thank you for everything!' I replied in astonishment,
'I didn't know that butterflies can talk,' it whispered back.
'Well now you know they can!'

The next morning I thought I'd had a magnificent dream. That afternoon I saw the butterfly, then I realised it wasn't a dream!

Aime-Leigh Blundell (9)
Marshside Primary School

A DAY IN THE LIFE OF LIONEL THE KITTEN

I woke up feeling hungry so I jumped up onto Mummy's side of the bed but decided to wake Pete up instead. Once I'd clambered over Mummy I started to lick Pete's face. He hadn't shaved since Monday and his bristles were prickly, so I licked his nose instead. He woke up and came downstairs to give me some food, then went back to bed.

I fell asleep in my little tray but was woken by Jack coming downstairs at eight. Soon I was in the house by myself. Suddenly I dashed outside and decided to climb the tree but when I reached the top, I felt worried. I tried to get down but my paw was stuck. I had to wait an hour before I eventually got down. My neighbour saw me stuck up the tree, he just shook his head as if I was mad. Then a strong wind blew the branch away from my paw and I jumped down.

After I'd had some food, I went upstairs to stalk the hamster. I looked at it in its wheel until it came out a little dizzy. Now it was time for action. I waggled my bum giving me accuracy. Then I swiped the cage while jumping and it toppled over with a crash!

Suddenly I felt a bit sleepy, so I went to my bed and curled up. Then I fell asleep and when my mum came in, she came straight upstairs and saw the hamster cage.

'Lionel!' she shouted, oh no, I was in trouble again.

Jack Donohoe (9)
Marshside Primary School

A Day In The Life Of A Puppy

I woke up from my normal night time sleep and I yawned a big yawn. I did a big stretch and started to walk towards the door and started to scratch at the door so Katie would come and open it for me. Just then Katie woke up and opened the door for me and then she went back to bed. I carefully went downstairs trying not to wake anybody up with my collar with the bell on it. When I got downstairs I ran into the kitchen, peered into my water bowl, thankfully there was some water in it, so I drank it all up. At that moment I saw next door's cat, I went through the flap in the door and started to chase him. I began to bark really loudly and that scared him away for good!

Next I heard someone calling my name so I turned round and saw Katie. I ran to her and she picked me up and stroked me so I gave her a big lick on the face. Katie took me into the house and put some food into my food bowl, I didn't eat any of it, I just ran into the living room and chewed on my chewy bone, it was very, very tasty. I carried my bone into the kitchen, I dropped it right in front of my food bowl and then ate my food. I went upstairs to my bed because I was really tired. So I curled up and fell fast asleep until the morning.

Katie Maddox (9)
Marshside Primary School

A DAY IN THE LIFE OF A BABY LION

I woke up one morning and I went to see my pet, Aslan. I gave him some water and food but I gave him humans' food instead of lions' food and then he shrunk! After, I was worrying because he was as small as an ant. He sat on the grass tired and sleepy.

I screamed to my mum upstairs, 'Mum, Aslan is as small as an ant because I gave him human food!'

Then he nearly got trodden on because he was plodding around everywhere and I didn't see him!

He started to lose his strength! My mum came down and she gasped as she saw Aslan lying on the floor.

'What's happened to poor Aslan?' Mum shouted.

Suddenly I trod on him, 'Oh no!' I shouted. He was dying now! I was really upset now because he was my close friend. A few moments went by and he was dead.

A few hours later I decided to give my lion a stroke on his back and all of a sudden he came back to life again.

'Hooray! Hooray! Hooray!' I yelled.

Meanwhile I went upstairs.

'Mum! Mum!' I shouted.

'Aslan has come back to life, his normal size, I am so glad!' Later I had tea and went to my cosy bed but I had to sleep with Aslan because I love him!

Georgia Preece (9)
Marshside Primary School

A DAY IN THE LIFE OF A LADYBIRD

I woke up with the bright morning sun and my son Eric came with me to look for food. A few hours later, in the afternoon, I called for Eric but he was nowhere to be seen.

'Eric, Eric, where are you?' I shouted.

The doors were open to the human's house, he must be in there I thought, so I dashed in.

The humans were having a party, it was like a nightmare! I looked in their kitchen on the side, in the cupboard. I looked in the oven but he wasn't there either. I looked in the spider's web but he wasn't there either.

But then, I realised I was stuck in the web. The spider was looking at me, I knew he was ready for the kill. He dived at me but I managed to move my body slightly and dodged the spider. He broke the web and set me free. I flew upstairs to look for him.

I checked the bathroom. I looked in the sink, the loo and the bath but he wasn't there either! 'Oh where could he be?' I moaned.

Drips of tears ran down my face, I was horrified, what could have happened to him? So I carried on looking for him. I checked the humans' mum's room. I travelled with my weak wings, searching the place for Eric. I saw a spider's web and there trapped was Eric. I dashed and escorted him to home.

'I'll never ever go on an adventure again!' explained Eric.

Michael Toby (9)
Marshside Primary School

A DAY IN THE LIFE OF A FLEA

One day I woke up and came into the kitchen. I jumped on it. He was going to the vet today. The dog got in his kennel, a lady took us to the car and locked us in.
I clambered out of the kennel thinking, 'I need some action.'
I went underneath the back seat and climbed up the door bravely, but when I got to jumping out I became scared. I jumped. Next thing I knew I'd hit a lamp post and flew backwards. (It felt like the traumatiser.) I went back underneath the back seat and started clambering up the kennel.

I fell down and found a hanky, tied it round me really hard for protection, climbed up again, the hanky was too thick to go through the hole. The door opened, a giant's hand came, I was terrified but it didn't harm me, I was surprised, it just lifted up the kennel, I fell out of the kennel but I parachuted down on the hanky. I looked around and jumped onto the path. I ran in-between the cracks in the path.

People were all over trying to squash me, so I quickly laid down and hid for a few minutes and suddenly I saw the lady I came with. I then bounced onto her leg, and with the hanky, climbed up her leg, tied the hanky on her pocket, got into the kennel and when we got home I took a nap on the dog. I woke up later, the dog was barking. I fell out of the window and died drowning in the pond.

Jonathan Rhodes (9)
Marshside Primary School

A Day In The Life Of Alfie Ant

Alfie Ant jumped out of bed, ran for the mail and a cup of coffee for his mum and dad. Alfie wobbled slowly upstairs with a tray full of cups, spoons, hot water, milk, saucers and the coffee jar. 'There's a letter here for you, I'll read it to you,' said Alfie's mum.

It said, 'You, Alfie Ant of Colony 12 have been chosen to find the lost treasure of Queen Victoriant. If found, return them to Colony Palace 12, 13.'

Alfie set off to find the first treasure, the amber mosquito, in Ant Creek Dungeon, it was hidden at three o'clock on the sea clock, the long hand of the clock is pointing at it.

The next treasure is her crown that was hidden in Ant Mine in five pieces. The first was on the track, the second on the roof, the third on the truck, the fourth on the ladder and the fifth on the generator.

The final treasure was the pear brooch in Tut Ant's tomb. It was in his sarcophagus, in his hand with a gold slab.

Miraculously Alfie, had found all the treasure he took them to Victoriant's palace and received a reward of six ant pounds of food for himself.

Maxwell Bowden (10)
Marshside Primary School

A Day In The Life Of My Dog Muttley

'Woof, woof, scratch, scratch, bang, bang!'
That's the sound of my dog Muttley when he wakes up at 6am (so I don't really need an alarm.) By the time my mum and me go to school and work he's off exploring the house doing things like destroying my mum's favourite plant, spreading the hamster's sawdust and rolling in it so he's covered in sawdust. Then my mum comes home for lunch, once she's cleaned everything up and has had her lunch she's off again, so he plays with my other dog boo. Once he's finished he takes a nap, when he wakes up it's time to destroy. Something like my bedroom door because he wants to get in but he won't accept the fact that the door is shut so he tries to drill through it with his claws. By now my mum and I have come home. We find him hiding in the kitchen because he's done something wrong, when he finds out that we're not angry he starts pouncing everywhere, knocking Boo flying. Now it's time for tea, but Boo seeks revenge! So as Muttley turns his back on his food it's gone!

Of course, we all know it was Boo, as Muttley gets a bone instead now after a hard day's work he goes to sleep.

Steven Basquill (10)
Marshside Primary School

A Day In The Life Of James The Giant

One sunny morning in Giant Land, James the giant was playing with some boulders. Suddenly, some little people, the giant's enemies came strolling up the hill with swords and shields ready to attack. Quick as a flash James rolled a boulder down the hill, it knocked two of the men flat but the army kept on marching up the hill.

So James rolled his second boulder and hit four more of the men over, but this didn't satisfy him so he picked up his biggest cane and tried swiping them, but the men just jumped over it. He carried on doing this and gradually tired the men out. He knocked them over and with superior power crushed them with a mallet.

He returned to his hillside home and told the giant's what had happened. They were furious and sent troops to invade the little people's town. They succeeded and took all the treasure and went back to their city. They rewarded James, for killing the first troop, generously.

Mark Coggins (9)
Marshside Primary School

A DAY IN THE LIFE OF ROGER THE DODGER

'Come on Roger,' shouted his dad.
'OK,' as he charged down the stairs like a herd of elephants.
'Breakfast's ready.'
'OK, OK,' said Roger as he reached the table.
'What's for breakfast Dad?' he asked.
'Toast.' said Dad.
'All right.'
'You've got a big day ahead of you.'
'What?' Roger exclaimed.
'A cross country race,' said Dad.

Later that day . . .
'Do I have to?' said Roger.
'Yes of course,' said Dad, 'it's only one mile.'
'A mile!' shouted Roger.
'I'll make a deal with you, Roger,' said Dad, 'you can do whatever you want for the rest of the day if you win.'
'OK!'

Five minutes later Roger was charging towards the finish line. He won first place. Dad, shouted liked something going bananas.
'Go, Roger, go!' shouted Dad.
He was awarded a trophy for coming first.

Alex Jenkins (10)
Marshside Primary School

A Day In The Life Of David Beckham

David Beckham is walking around Southport, with his wife Victoria.
Soon he is in town. I am travelling on the bus to meet him.

David said, 'I am playing at Anfield against Liverpool! Are you coming
to watch?'
'Yes please,' I replied and then I added, 'Can I have your autograph?'
'Yes, here you are!' he said, 'See you there.'
Arrived at the training field, ran to his manager.
'Hello, David, start training, quickly we finish in two minutes!'
'Can I have a shot at Fabien Barthez?' he asked.
Alex agreed. Beckham looked at the ball, decided where to shoot and
scored. It was a brilliant goal. Training ended.

'We are just starting a match, Liverpool Vs Manchester United!'
announced the commentator.
The kick-off is taken by Heskey and Fowler, first they attack and
Michael Owen passes to Fowler who passes back to Michael Owen,
Owen scores. It's 1-0 to Liverpool. Brilliant! Next, David passes to
Ryan Giggs, but Owen intercepts and kicks the ball out, it's a corner!
Beckham takes the corner, passes to Giggs and scores with a header. It's
1-1! The whistle blows for half-time.

In the second half Giggs and David kick off, with one minute to go,
Alex Ferguson congratulates the Manchester United football team on
their 2-1 victory.

Lavinia Norton (9)
Marshside Primary School

A DAY IN THE LIFE OF FRED THE RED CORNSNAKE

It was another dull and normal day for myself, Fred the red cornsnake, slithering in my old and unchanged wooden cage, but my only excitement was that I was about to shed my skin.

Exactly five hours later I woke up and went to see if I could find a mouse. I was looking for five minutes when the top of the cage opened, then I rushed as fast as a living snake could go under my terracotta pot. As soon as I heard the lid click back into place I got back out and had another look for a mouse. I found one. It was in a corner of the cage so I sneaked up quickly and quietly so it couldn't see or hear me. I swallowed it whole. It was extremely tasty.

The next day I woke and found my skin was wobbily so I rubbed myself against my water tub. It was a squash, a squeeze and a struggle to get out but I did. After that I went to sleep, an hour later I woke up, because I was cold, so I tried to get back in my skin, but I got stuck in it, so I tried as hard as I could but I couldn't budge, then my owner came back to see how I was. The next thing I knew I was at the vet. The vet cut the back half of the skin off and then cut the skin that was on me in half with a special pair of scissors. Minutes later I was back in my cage.

Sam Wragg (9)
Marshside Primary School

A Day In The Life Of The Prime Minister's Daughter

'Brrrrrrng!' My butler Mr McMillen came rushing in and switched my alarm clock off. I bounded out of my four poster bed. I heard Bobby, Mum's maid, go to attend to my baby sister Flick!

While I was getting dressed Mum came in and said, 'I'm leaving you in charge today, Auntie Kerry's made a mess of her paper work and has asked me to go and help and I've got to go now! So good luck, see you soon!'

Everything was running smoothly until I donated £500,000 to a company that made chocolate bars whose proceeds support the fight against cancer. To my utter horror, a few days later the company had sold lots of chocolate bars and made lots of money, but caused an outbreak of an unknown illness. Hospitals throughout England were chocka with people with a mysterious illness. Some even had to close to stop entry of more sick people! What could I do?

After careful thought I rang a scientist to help! The next few days were difficult for everyone, we got letters and phone calls of complaints until finally the scientist, Mr Waltz, declared on the national news at nine that it didn't look like the chocolate caused the illness. Two days later it was proved, Mr Waltz was right.

Soon after Mum arrived home she said I'd done so well she might leave me in charge of the country again but I said, 'No way!'

Jordan Swainson (10)
Marshside Primary School

A Day In The Life Of A Tea Cup

It was morning and Mum was busy making breakfast for Dad. Sparkle the spoon waited until the coast was clear then hopped out of the open drawer onto the floor. Eventually she reached the shelf, in which her friends Cathy the cup and Susie the saucer were waiting.

'At last, you're here!' said Cathy.
'We've been waiting for ages,' said Susie.
A door upstairs banged. They all jumped with surprise, stomp, stomp, Dad was coming downstairs in a cross and grumpy mood, as if he'd had a huge row with Mum. They froze in horror, as Dad snatched them up and put them in a small box. With the box, he ran out the door, down the street into his lab. He just wanted to experiment on them.

Finally he reached the lab. Cathy, Susie and Sparkle were having a little doze when they were roughly woken by a strange noise.
'Brumm, brumm, brumm,' went the machine.
'Where are we?' said Susie with surprise.
'What's going on,' questioned Cathy and Sparkle together.
They were in the place taker, time machine. Then they vanished.

They reappeared in outer space, twisting and turning with a loud crash, they landed in Pot and Pan Land. All the pots and pans greeted them warmly, although they were such an evil bunch. They planned many entertainments to stop them going home.
'Come to our carnival, it'll be so gloomy without you,' the pans pleaded hopefully while the pots sniggered quietly.
'Sorry, we must be going,' replied Sparkle quickly.
Sparkle knew their plan . . .

Emma Legge (10)
Marshside Primary School

A Day In The Life Of Antony The Ant

As soon as the sun went up, Antony shot out of bed to get an early start on collecting food for the lavish bouquet that was set to take place that afternoon. There were ants coming from colonies all around the world to see the king's daughter's birthday celebrations. Antony was extremely busy collecting food for the banquet. He blew the horn, to wake up all the collector ants.

After a few hours of searching they returned with a beautiful supply of goodies. The banquet started, with a choir of bugs playing a song as the royal party walked towards their table. When the king gave the signal everyone started to tuck into their food. Suddenly, all of the lights went out and everyone went quiet.

After a few minutes, Antony stood up and went to the entrance to see what was going on. He saw a stone blocking the way of the hole, he tried to move it but it was too big for him to lift. All the other ants got up and began to help him, but it was useless.

One of Antony's friends came up to him and said, 'I'm small enough to fit through that hole there, I could go and get Maurice the mole to dig us out.'

'That's a good idea, but you be careful.' he squeezed through the small gap and found Maurice. After a few hours, they returned. He got started straight away, within a few hours she'd dug them out. Maurice was the hero!

Curtis Evans (10)
Marshside Primary School

A Day In The Life Of Michael Atherton

I shot out of bed excited about going to my first cricket match ever. I was meeting my team mates at Old Trafford in Lancashire. I was on my way to my first match, I was two hours away.

Suddenly, I heard noises from my limousine and just then it stopped. The car had run out of petrol. So I ran as fast as I could to the nearest petrol station, it took half an hour to get there and back. The driver had to go top speed in the limo, we just made it to the match for 9.15am and I had to be there for 9.20am. The game started immediately. I was in bat first against Curtly Ambrose. I hit the ball for a six followed by a single. Alec Stewart was in bat and he did a sweep shot and that went for a four.

It was the end of the over and we'd got nine runs off the over. I was in bat and I hit the ball right at one post of the stadium and quarter of the stadium fell down. I was really disappointed but they soon got it fixed and then Jimmy Adams and Brian Lara, but they didn't get any more, we got 409 runs but Pakistan only 403, so we won by five runs.

Scott Littler (10)
Marshside Primary School

A DAY IN THE LIFE OF SPIKE THE CAT

It was one very ordinary day and Spike had set off to the country. He was a very adventurous cat, he liked to be on his feet all day exploring. He went past a big field but suddenly he turned back to explore it further.

He was digging in the bushes, and he was having great fun. He moved on up to the trees with huge trunks so he could climb up them. He reached the top and he could see the whole field it was absolutely astonishing. It was too big to be true. Spike looked at the apple green grass, it was the loveliest colour of grass he had ever seen.

Spike caught sight of another cat, he zoomed down the tree and ran to where the other cat was sitting. He was so mad that the cat had come onto the field that he was playing on. Spike was so cross that he started to scrap. Before long they were still scrapping and were covered in scratches and bruises. Things were really getting out of hand but they didn't care! They were close to breaking each other's limbs but fortunately they didn't.

Suddenly, he stopped, he crushed some berries under his paw. A strange purple haze appeared and he looked at Crackers, the cat he was fighting, she was the prettiest cat he'd ever seen, he had fallen in love with her. He must have crushed the magical berries, who knows? But from that day on, they never split up. They were inseparable.

Kerry McFadzean (10)
Marshside Primary School

A DAY IN THE LIFE OF A DUSTBIN MAN

It was just an ordinary day for Bill the dustbin man, he was collecting the rubbish from Newbank Road in Southmead. He came up to the largest house in the road. He collected the rubbish and zoomed off down the road. When he arrived at the tip he went into the staffroom and made himself a coffee. 'Bring, bring, bring' bring!' It was the phone.

'Oh that dratted thing,' complained Bill. He answered it, it was Mrs Little saying she'd lost her valuable brown fur coat.

Bill thought he should start looking straight away, but he couldn't be bothered so he finished his drink and then he began his search.

He looked for an hour and still couldn't find it. He asked Fred his mate to help him.

They hunted for most of the afternoon then Bill said, 'It's nearly 4 o'clock we can go home,' they both went to get their coats from the staffroom when Sam came in holding something.

'What are you doing with that Sam?' Bill asked curiously.

'I found this coat and I thought I'd take it home for my wife,' said Sam looking pleased with himself.

'You can't take that, it belongs to Mrs Little!'

Bill told Sam the whole story and when he'd finished explaining Bill looked in the pockets and found a diamond ring.

'OK Fred, we better go.'

But Fred had already gone, Bill phoned Mrs Little and told her he would be round in five minutes. When he arrived she took the coat and gave him a £100 reward.

Joanne Wilson (10)
Marshside Primary School

A DAY IN THE LIFE OF A GRASSHOPPER

Sam was a very adventurous grasshopper and he had a good friend called Harry the wasp. 'Hey, I'm going out for a while,' Harry shouted to Sam.

'All right,' replied Sam. The door slammed, Sam was reading the newspaper.

A few hours later, Harry had not returned, Sam guessed that a spider in the spiders' village had caught him. He rushed out and saw the bright green grass and blue flowers but Harry was nowhere to be seen. He found his friend Max the mantis soon after they were in the spiders' village.

Straight away they saw Harry, 'Help!' he shouted. Max flew up and cut the web. Harry came down to help Sam and Max. He zoomed down at a spider and stung it. Fortunately after that all the spiders ran off. That night everybody had a big celebration that had golden fireworks and silver sparklers when it started to rain everybody went to the pub Sam, Max and Harry had some beer and had a long chat with Bill the beetle. The pub owner then went home and watched some TV about human pets and their dangers, then collapsed into bed and fell asleep after their eventful day.

Jeffrey Byrne (9)
Marshside Primary School

A DAY IN THE LIFE OF TYCHO

In deep space, far into the future there was a battle-scarred warrior and his companion. Tycho, the battle scarred warrior and his companion Moriar, the chosen, were playing battle darts. Battle darts is like normal darts but the players use darts that have minute rocket boosters. There was a knock at the door.

'Who is it?' Tycho asked as he threw his favourite dart carelessly. Suddenly the door was smashed down and hundreds of death troopers stormed in and destroyed their apartment! Tycho fought his way through to get out of the determined army.

Tycho shot off on his hover board, to find people who could help him to rescue Moriar from the huge prison on Zidane. Tycho knew that that's where he would be because that's where the death troopers always took their falsely accused victims. Tycho borrowed a light speed space shuttle (LSSS) and zoomed across the galaxy.

He landed in a clearing in a dense jungle, when he got out of the LSSS hundreds of honour troops came out from the trees. Tycho explained why he was there. The honour troops said that they would help Tycho free Moriar if he could find the asteroid Dane's centre core which was extremely valuable.

Tycho went to a souvenir shop to be a fake one but an honour guard warrior, guarded the shop so he had to make the long journey to find it. He got it with the hope of rescuing his friend. Tycho and the honour troops completed the rescue mission successfully.

Christopher Brownley (10)
Marshside Primary School

A Day In The Life Of Two Twin Sisters Anna And Hannah

'Hannah, get up, breakfast is being served,' shouted Anna. She stretched and yawned, a second later the alarm clock went off, 'Beep, beep, beep'. Anna screwed her hand up into a fist and hit the off button. It fell on the floor and broke, the pieces scattered everywhere.

'It doesn't matter, it's only a stupid alarm clock.' Hannah shouted.
'At least it wakes you up lazy.' Anna stomped down the stairs in a mood.
'Here is your breakfast.'
'Where?'
'Nowhere because there is none left, I've eaten it.'
'Grab your coat we are going to the park,' said Hannah rather quickly as she rushed off,

The park was very quiet, until a dog started barking. The dog was upset. Soon they discovered it was a girl. The dog didn't appear to have an owner. So the girls took the dog home. They pleaded and begged their parents to let them keep it.
'Why don't you take the dog out on your trip to the museum, whilst Dad and I decide what to do. But put posters up first,' Mum said in the kind of way that made us think she had already made the right decision. They put twenty-four posters up asking if people had lost a dog.
'Finished at last,' Anna said, 'finally we can go to the museum.' But they could not find the dog, they wandered off looking for it. They ran in a hurry all the way home to tell Mum. To their surprise, Mum was with the dog!
'You can keep him,' she said laughing.

Hannah Miller (10)
Marshside Primary School

A Day In The Life Of Van Nistilroy

'So are you going to sign or what?' demanded Sir Alex Ferguson.

'Yes!' replied Manchester United's newest recruit, Van Nistilroy. A second later, all the newspaper editors came bursting through the door and started bombarding him with all sorts of questions.

After the signing he was exhausted and collapsed into bed although he couldn't get to sleep. His dogs Marco and Rolo jumped on his bed and started pouncing around.

The following morning, he picked up his breakfast from Mojo's breakfast store and soon after, he was travelling to Old Trafford to play Leeds in the Champion's League. Unfortunately Van didn't play.

Alex phoned up Van and said, 'You've got to play,' luckily he scored but at the same time he broke his leg. He was in such agony, he started crying.

He was rushed to hospital, his fibula and tibia were broken. He couldn't play for at least twelve weeks. He was so frightened by the experience he didn't want to play football again. Slowly, over the next few years he wanted to play again. He missed the excitement of the game. He played for his country, then started playing for Celtic and his life became successful once more.

Andrew Watts (10)
Marshside Primary School

A DAY IN THE LIFE OF CHRISTOPHER BLAKE

'Come on Chris, you'll be late,' said Mum.

'Alright, I know it's swimming,' he said cheerfully. He was practising for the school swimming gala next Tuesday along with his fellow team mates. He was a very good swimmer and did not need to practise but he still practised every day, he was very dedicated.

The great day had arrived, Chris was ready and so were all of his team mates but he was wondering where Liam was because he had been in school that day. Then he heard the phone ring, it was Liam's mum he had broken his arm and could not swim anymore. Mr Wright asked if any body wanted to take his place but no one would.

Chris said, 'OK, I will take his place,' so Chris entered the race and won it. He and his team won the relay and won the cup for the best swimming team in the entire gala. Liam was pleased to hear about the news and recovered six weeks later.

The following months they had entered a competition along with fifty other schools in the area initially they did not do very well but suddenly they started to win a lot of races. They won the championship and took the cup home to celebrate. They gave the cup to Chris and he took it to his study. He showed it to his parents and they were so pleased they called all the family over to have a party and celebrated his victory.

Christopher Blake (9)
Marshside Primary School

A Day In The Life Of Three Creepy Crawlies

In the trees of someone's house, there were three creepy crawlies who didn't get on, well actually two of them did. They were called William the wasp, Fred the fly and Sam the spider. Each day William and Fred went out to explore the garden, but one day they were unfortunate.

When they were going out Fred was extremely careless and got caught in one of Sam's webs! Fred instantly called to William for help. William struggled to help his friend, but after a while said to Sam, 'Why are we fighting when we could be playing together happily?'
'You've got a point there William. Why are we fighting? I shall free Fred at once so we can play and have adventures together,' declared Sam.

Sam freed Fred in an instant and the three of them went to the house to explore, but they didn't know that the people who were inside hated crawlies and had pesticides that would kill any bug on earth.

When they were in the house they used their best stealth techniques to avoid being seen because they could hear voices close by. They could see many pesticides and fly swatters but as they were gazing at them somebody spotted the friends and started swiping at them with a swatter as fast as lightning.

They instantly went for the gap in a door where they came in and went straight to the rockery at the end of the garden. They found a little gap under a rock and quickly rushed under. They were safe, for now!

Liam Parkes (9)
Marshside Primary School

A DAY IN THE LIFE OF MY SISTER ASHLEY

One morning at 6,30am twins Sarah and Ashley woke up to a golden sun shining through the window.

'I just thought you might like to know, you slept in a bed with a spider in it,' giggled Sarah.

Ashley jumped out of the bed with an ear-piercing scream. 'Come on then, let's go and get breakfast,' said Ashley angrily.

As they went downstairs, Ashley pushed Sarah along. When they were at the bottom, Sarah asked what was for breakfast, as if she was hungry. Her stomach started to rumble.

'Excuse my stomach,' giggled Sarah.
'We've got bacon and eggs, what would you like?' asked Mum.
'Bacon and eggs please,' said the twins.

After they'd finished they went and got dressed.

'Come on girls,' shouted Dad.

They put the dog and the surfboards into the car and drove off. When they got to the beach Sarah and Ashley ran with the surfboards into the water and hit a wave. Meanwhile, Mum and Dad were sunbathing and the dog was wandering around. Sarah passed Ashley a water gun. She said, 'I bet I can get you off the surfboard.'
'All right, you've got a bet.'

They put water in the guns and started to squirt each other. Mum shouted them to get the dog.

'We'll go and look for her,' they said.

They looked in the bushes, down holes and in the water but they couldn't find her, then they heard a bark. They went looking near their mum's sun bed and there she was.

Sarah Earle (10)
Marshside Primary School

131

A Day In The Life Of Tigger The Cat And His Friends

Tigger's owner, Karen, opened the back door and Tigger ran out to play. He saw Kitty and Buster chasing a butterfly. When he saw the butterfly he followed it too.

'Miaow!' said Tigger.
'Tigger, you're not in the house, you can talk now,' replied Kitty.
'Oh yeah!'

They kept on chasing the butterfly until they reached Botanic Gardens. All three of them strolled into the entrance and went for a play.

'Be careful on this bridge,' said Buster strictly. All the kittens slowly walked across. With one slip of the foot Kitty fell into the lake. Tigger, an excellent swimmer, jumped into the lake and put Kitty on his back. Tigger was doing a great job swimming with his little legs.

While Tigger was putting all his effort into rescuing Kitty, Buster was getting bored so he decided to go for a walk. Buster was the silly one of the group and always got himself lost, this time he got himself stuck in a dark, black hole.

A man spotted the two kittens, Tigger and Kitty, lying down puffing. He picked them up and took them to the café.

'Miaow!' said Kitty.

Whilst he phoned the RSPCA, Buster arrived.

'Hi.'
'Where have you been?'
'Oh, I got stuck in a hole.'

A man arrived to collect the kittens. They drove up the drive of the RSPCA and two nurses came to collect them from the van. They put the cats on the table and checked their microchips and they were all taken home safe and well.

Emma Hunt (10)
Marshside Primary School

A DAY IN THE LIFE OF CLINE MY RABBIT

'Come on, breakfast is here,' called Cline.
'Hang on a minute, I'm just making the bed,' came a reply.

Calvin and Cline tucked into their rabbit food.

'Here I am,' shouted Fudge and she burst in with straw and newspaper all over her.
'What happened to you?' laughed Miriam closing the hutch door.

Fudge had a big stretch, but in the process of doing so she tipped over the bowl of food, getting lettuce stuck in her claws.

'It isn't a good day for you, is it Mum?' chuckled Calvin eating the lettuce.

Cline was lazing about when the latch clicked and the door opened.
'Oh, it's just Miriam,' Cline said to herself and went back to sleep.

When she woke up she found herself lying in Miriam's back garden. She started hopping about looking for Fudge and Calvin. They were nowhere to be seen. Cline soon started bobbing around on the road. After a while she got lost, on the motorway!

Cline jumped onto a trailer, she was shaking like a leaf. After a few hours the trailer whizzed past a street she knew. She leapt bravely off the trailer onto the pavement and jumped away. She pounced back home. When she got inside Miriam strolled out. Calvin and Fudge were following.

'A cat had opened the latch and we dragged you away,' whispered Fudge calmly to Cline.
'At least we're back together,' Cline sighed.

Esther Fullwood (10)
Marshside Primary School

A Day In The Life Of Percy

Percy was hopping around until he saw Rose the ladybird. She was crying.

'What's up Rose?' said Percy.
'I've lost my family,' replied Rose unhappily.
'When did you last see them?' asked Percy.

Rose told him she last saw them at home but when she went for a walk it began to get windy and Rose blew away. Percy and Rose went on a walk. Rose remembered the blueberry tree.

'So we go right, don't we?' said Percy.

He led the way. Rose flew around a little while Percy was sniffing. He found a long trail of footprints like a caterpillar's. They followed the caterpillar's trail and ended up at a dead end. Rose found a den she had made, they sat down on the grass and played 'I Spy'.

Eventually Rose fell asleep and Percy carried her on her favourite leaf. He walked slowly so she would not fall off. Percy looked round then he stood on Rose's special stick and found the oak tree where Rose played with her brother and sister. Then a cool breeze came and woke Rose up.

Rose said, 'I can see owl's house so go straight ahead.'

Then they met Robin the bird. 'Hello Percy and Rose, what's up?' asked Robin.
'Rose has lost her family,' answered Percy.
'I will help you find them,' said Robin.

Robin flew in the air and went straight on. He saw, from above, Rose's brother and sister. Robin came swooping down excitedly and said he had seen her brother and sister. Rose leapt on Robin's back and they set off. Percy followed them on the ground. When they reached Rose's home everyone was pleased to see her. Percy and Robin left feeling proud and happy.

Rebecca Golder (10)
Marshside Primary School

A Day In The Life Of Britney Spears

I was in my room brushing my hair, singing a Britney Spears song and wishing I was Britney. And then, as if by magic, I was on stage with a crowd all around me. I looked at myself in amazement, in astonishment. I looked just like Britney Spears, my wish had come true.

It was great. I sounded like her too. Two directors came to me and asked if I was ready for my tour. I said 'Yes!' I was really excited by this time.

A week later

Now I was really getting used to being Britney, but it was so tiring. The most sleep I had was five hours. I didn't know when the tour was finishing but what I did know was we were making a video.

Fancy that, me in a video as Britney Spears in a month's time. Then I thought it's my birthday in three weeks. Loads of images ran through my head. What if I don't get back in time? What if the real Britney gets all my presents and I don't get any? Just imagine, a birthday with no presents, it would be dreadful.

Three weeks had nearly gone by - it was my birthday the next day, so I decided to go to sleep.

It was my birthday and I was at home opening my presents. I was so relieved I went and hugged my mum and dad. At least I could have my birthday with my family, and Britney could do her video too.

Nicola Kenyon (10)
Middlewich Primary School

A Day In The Life Of Andrew Spot

I walked down the long, gloomy hall. I thought of my next lesson, it was spells. I liked it sometimes, but not today, as it was *bad* spells and something always goes wrong.

When I spoke to my parents later that day they asked me what I had done.
I replied, 'We were doing spells and I didn't enjoy them.'

We never did literacy, sometimes I wished I wasn't a wizard because every day we did the same.

A couple of weeks later we broke up for the holiday. This I enjoyed more than anything else.

I went to a nearby park where I played on the swings. I saw a large blue pond. There was a shimmer of orange and gold. I wondered what it could be. Then as I peered around a massive brown oak tree I saw a man fishing with a green spotted rod. As I swung back and forth the man had vanished. There was no trace of him ever being there.

There was a sudden gust of wind which made me revolve in circles. I lost my balance and plummeted towards the grassy ground. I struggled to my feet and the man was standing in front of me. He was old with grey hair and enormous blue eyes. A cap was perched on his head. He spoke to me in a gruff voice. 'What are you doing?'
'I am playing,' I replied in a shaky voice.
'Oh!'

The old man picked me up and dusted me off. That's when my adventure began . . .

Lewis Bertoni (10)
Middlewich Primary School

A DAY IN THE LIFE OF MY DAD

I get up at 6.00am and take the twins downstairs. I give them milk, then make packed lunches for school and work. Then I go to the bathroom and get dressed, then I go to work.

When I get to Willow Lodge Gatehouse I disinfect my car and shoes against foot and mouth. I drive up to the hall where I work. When I get to work I unlock the greenhouses and open all the vents and feed the cat. I collect the tools I will need for the jobs I have to do in the morning. The jobs I do change with the weather and time of the year. Jobs could include planting plants and trees, changing bedding plants, pruning, weeding, tree felling, grass cutting, watering and sowing seeds. The list is a small part of what gardeners do.

When it rains I work in the greenhouses sowing seeds and taking cuttings to grow more plants to plant in the gardens. When it's sunny and dry we all work outside, in and around the gardens and hall. There are four gardeners where I work and we look after sixteen acres of gardens. I do not have a normal day because things that grow are always changing. They will always need looking after and care.

Robert Groom (10)
Middlewich Primary School

A Day In The Life Of A One Pound Coin

6.30am - (Inside a moneybox) Every coin and note woke up within half an hour.

7.00am - Suddenly the lid of the moneybox opens and a gigantic hand takes out £4 and reaches in again to take out a £1 coin, and then shuts the lid.

7.10am - (Inside boy's pocket at the candy store) The boy wants to buy some sweets which cost £4.50. The boy takes out all his pound coins and 50p.

1.30pm - (Inside the till) The shop owner drops the cash till and all the money falls out. A little kid picks up the £1 coin and puts it in his pocket.

3.00pm - (Inside a moneybox) The moneybox falls over. A dog picks up the £1 coin and puts it in his kennel.

5.30pm - (Inside the dog kennel) The little kids mom is changing the blankets in the dog's kennel and she comes across the £1 coin, so she slips it into her pocket and continues changing the blankets.

5.45pm - (On the streets of New York) The little kid's mom, on her way to the bank, went past a sewage drain, then the £1 coin dropped out of her pocket and into the drain.

7.00pm - (In New York sewers) The £1 coin got carried through the sewers and finally made it to the sea where he drifted back to England.

The next day the boy at the start found him.

Adam Hough (10)
Middlewich Primary School

A Day In The Life Of Kian Of Westlife

I woke up, I was on the double bed. Nicky was on the single bed, Bryan on the fold-up bed, Shane was on the sofa and Mark was on the floor. It was 5.00am and tonight at 7.00pm we have to see our band manager.

I was up first. I had two slices of toast and then I woke Nicky, Bryan, Shane and Mark. We decided to call our band 'Westlife'. The reason we called ourselves this is because we all lived in the west and we are the life. Our band manager also thought it was a good name.

We have a concert and we are going to sing 'Uptown Girl', 'Fool Again', 'My Love', 'When You're Looking Like That', 'Dreams Come True' and 'I Lay My Love On You'.

That night we went to the Manchester Evening News Arena to do the concert. I was so nervous. The concert was brilliant. Afterwards we went back to our hotel. Mark was the first to go to sleep, then Shane, then Bryan, then Nicky and then at last me.

That was my day.

Zoe Evans (10)
Middlewich Primary School

A DAY IN THE LIFE OF SABRINA

I woke up in a good mood. I got dressed in the halter-top I bought yesterday. (I'm tempted to buy the pink one too!) I thought the day would get worse. How wrong was I? When I got to school we had double history, my favourite. We all had a *big* test. I think I did quite well actually.

It seemed like hours till lunchtime. As soon as the bell rang I quickly went to the cafeteria. Today is Wednesday so we get the yummy food.

Harvey came over to sit with me. He asked me if I wanted to go to the slicery with him. I soon said yes.

When school had finished I met up with Harvey. He said to meet at 7.00pm. The time quickly passed by. I put my most gorgeous pink nail varnish and lip-gloss on. (My motto is 'think pink'.)

When Harvey and I got to the slicery we saw Libby with Jill and Cee-cee. Libby called me a 'freak' as usual but we just ignored them and ordered. I overheard Libby talking about me so when Jill and Cee-cee went to the cloakroom I turned her into a frog. She soon leapt away. When Jill and Cee-cee came back they went outside to look for Libby. Harvey and I just ate. When we had finished he walked me home. I said goodnight and went in. Aunt Hilda and Zelda didn't notice me so I went straight up to bed.

Gemma Bailey (10)
Middlewich Primary School

A DAY IN THE LIFE OF BART SIMPSON AND FAMILY

One day my dad woke me up and said, 'We are going to a dinosaur museum today Bart, do you want to come?'
I said, 'Hi caramba, yes certainly Dad!'

So we set off and when we got there I ran in quicker than you can say 'Eat my shorts.' Dad, Mom, Lisa and Maggie all went into the museum and I said, 'Gee-wiz, this is big! And I mean big!'

We went round the museum and Maggie knocked down a dinosaur skeleton, by pulling one of its leg bones from under it. We couldn't see her anywhere. The skeleton had fallen on top of her.

Dad and Mom called the security guard who called the curator (the boss of the museum.)

'My little daughter has been attacked by your vicious dinosaur,' shouted Dad.
'Don't be stupid mon,' shouted the curator, Willie. 'Your wee girl knocked it doon and you can't go home until you've rebuilt it.'

Dad, Mom, Lisa and me started to rummage through the pile on bones and tried to rebuild the dinosaur and when we got to the bottom of the pile Maggie was still not there!

What I didn't know was that Santa's Little Helper (our dog) had sneaked in with us, grabbed a dinosaur leg bone and ran off down the corridor with the dinosaur crashing down behind him and with Maggie following him down the corridor knocking over ancient Ming vases, armless statues and glass cases of Egyptian relics. She followed him down the stairs into the basement into a room full of dusty old packing cases, this is where we found her, and she was perfectly safe!

Dad thought that we should make a quick escape so we ran away through the nearest fire escape. We got straight into the car and drove back to our home in Springfield.

Peter Daniel (10)
Middlewich Primary School

A DAY IN THE LIFE OF A HIPPOPOTAMUS IN A GAME RESERVE IN SOUTH AFRICA

One hot summer's day in Africa I was sitting in a nice, cool dam with my family and friends. At the water's edge were a family of turtles all swimming and playing. Above them was a viewing hide and people were sitting in it. They sit there hour after hour watching the animals and taking photographs of us.

After a long, restful day under the water with just my eyes and nose showing I come up for air every few minutes.

When the sun had gone down I crept out of the water in my usual foot printed muddy path. This one night a white rhino was heading straight towards me on my path. I charged it. It charged back. We hit each other in anger and fright and both screamed in pain. I gave the rhino a right good hit in the side, he fell to the ground. I thought I had won the fight but he got back up and looked at me with fear in his eyes. I stood my ground and waited for him to charge. I got up and started at him. After fighting for about an hour he eventually backed up to the bushes and walked to the other side of the dam.

He only wanted a drink of water, but us hippos always stick to the path.

Catherine Fallows (10)
Middlewich Primary School

THE GLADIATOR'S LIFE

Gladiators fight usually in the Coliseum. Sometimes slaves are forced to fight, their weapon is a sword. A Gladiator's life is a hard life. Gladiators always get hurt and injured and a whole day will be a hard life.

The Gladiator's Day

The army first get ready in the arena, then the day begins. He wonders what will come out for him to fight. The army attacked and they were Gladiators on chariots and Gladiators themselves.

They had an army of slaves. Maximus told the slaves what to do. They were ready for battle; they got their swords out and fought for their lives. Slaves died that day. The Gladiators fought to kill the two slaves. Maximus was angry so chopped one of the Gladiator's heads off in the helmet. Now the battle began. He killed a Gladiator and got the chariot from him. He chopped most of the Gladiators feet off. Then Maximus defied an Emperor. When he saw Maximus had now he didn't show his face or say his name but he did in the end after the Emperor saw him he knew who he was. It was Maximus, the General of the Roman Army. Maximus had a new job as *Gladiator.*

Dean Johnson (9)
Nenthead Primary School

A Day In The Life Of Pansy

One day Pansy the kitten was woken by the sound of a tiny mouse running across the kitchen floor. Up jumped Pansy and chased the mouse out the kitchen, past the pile of clean washing, knocking it over on his way past, out the cat flap, through the garden and over the bridge which goes over the river.

Pansy carried on chasing the mouse for a very long time, but at last the mouse came to its home. Pansy started to go back the way he had come, but when he got back to the river he forgot about the bridge and he thought he was stuck.

While he was stuck, it was his dinner time and the girl was going to feed her, but she didn't know where Pansy was. The girl went to tell her mum that she couldn't find Pansy and that she needed help to find her. The girl and her mum looked in every place you could imagine. They were just about to give up looking for Pansy when they heard a miaow. They followed the sound of the little kitten until they were standing right in front of him. Mum took him back to the house. Mum and the girl fed Pansy then she fell fast asleep on the bed.

Sarah Herdman (8)
Nenthead Primary School

A DAY IN THE LIFE OF STELLA

Through the hole shone sunlight, like a piercing laser, it caught my eye. I woke up, startled by a loud noise buzzing behind the wall. Petrified by shooting holes of light through the wall, I ran and ran out of my house and across the soft carpet. I could still hear the blaring of the machine so I kept running right under a strange wall. I stopped dead. The weird sound had gone. Ahead lay a forest, gigantic with wonderful trees and leaves in all the colours of the rainbow.

I took a tiny step forward and fell down and down, eventually landing in the forest. All the trees looked the same but in darker and lighter shades. They had no trunk, just grew straight up. I was enchanted. Suddenly I heard footsteps, eight of them in all, making a tremendous sound. It was coming towards me. I couldn't move. Out emerged a huge, black spider. I had seen them in pictures. Its red, evil eyes were staring right at me.

'What are you staring at?' the spider snarled gruffly.
'My name is erm . . . Stella,' I answered. trembling. 'I'm a stag beetle and erm . . . I'm trying to find my way home.'
'Mmm, I'm Spencer and I'd be happy to help,' murmured the spider, not so scary now. 'You just turn around and you can't miss the house.'
'Thank you so much Spencer, you're so kind.'
'That's OK,' he replied and stamped off mumbling to himself.

I think I had been walking for about ten hours when I saw an amazing sight. All around me were the strange and brilliant trees I had seen earlier - red and orange, yellow and blue. But, one in particular was outstanding. It was pale pink and so tall it almost touched the sky. On the top was the most beautiful thing I have ever seen, a butterfly as white as a cloud, I could almost feel its silky wings. All of a sudden it came fluttering down like feather. It stood out against the sun.

'Hi, I'm Stella the stag beetle and I was wondering if you could fly up if I'm near the house.'
'But you're nowhere near, you've been going in the wrong direction,' kindly said the wonderful butterfly.
'But . . . but I took directions from a spider,' I had started to worry. 'Was that by any chance Spencer?'

'Yes, why?'

'Every bug knows he's evil,' answered the butterfly. 'You're not from around here are you?'

'No, I live in the house.'

'You poor thing, I'm Bryony. You just go in the other direction, but it's getting late, do you want to come home with me?' questioned Bryony.

'No, I've got to get home,' I replied with determination.

'OK. I might see you around,' and she flew away, now out of sight.

I turned around and set off back home. I couldn't wait.

I was getting really tired but I was sure I was nearly home. All of a sudden the ground started to shake. I could hear laughing as I fell onto my back. I was petrified as I heard a scream.

'Emily, what is it?' asked another girl's voice.

'A . . . a bug!' answered Emily.

'Don't worry, I'll get it.'

Squash, squish, squelch - that was the end of my day.

Katy Jones (11)
Nenthead Primary School

A Day In The Life Of An Animal - A Green Bottle

A green bottle is a fly. It has big, red, bold eyes. Its body is green and its wings are kind of see-through. It eats rotten plants. The sun wakes the green bottle up in the morning. He flies around into exciting places like in the gardens, finding rotten plants. An owl eats a green bottle. An owl comes out when it gets dark, so the green bottle better watch out!

One day Keeley was in the garden when she saw a green bottle. The green bottle was massive, it was bigger than a usual fly but Keeley just carried on gardening. The green bottle didn't like Keeley pulling out the rotten plants.

The green bottle flew away and Keeley went to her friend, Laura. Keeley told Laura about the green bottle. Laura said, 'Wow! Where is it now?'
'I don't know. I was gonna take it in my house but it flew away.'

The green bottle was already in Keeley's house because she left the kitchen window open and it was biting into the fruit. When Keeley and Laura got home they saw that there was tiny little holes in the bananas, oranges and apples, and all of the grapes where gone. Laura said, 'The green bottle must have got in the kitchen window because it is open.'
'So where do you think it is now?'
'I think I know,' said Laura. 'Have you got any plants in your house?'
'Yes I have, in my bedroom and Mum's room.'
'We better go in your room to see if it's there.'

It was eating the rotten bits of her plant. Keeley said, 'Laura, go and get the fly spray!'
'OK!' said Laura. So she ran downstairs to get the fly spray from the cupboard and then quickly ran upstairs again.
'Squirt it at him then Laura.'

So she did, but she missed then she squirted it again. She got him this time. She put it down the sink.

Catrina Hainsworth (10)
Nenthead Primary School

A Day In The Life Of Sharon

For the last couple of weeks Sharon, the sea horse, had been playing with her friends and family. Playing passy with the pebbles and skipping with the seaweed. But not today, today nobody was around, not even her best friends the fish, Frank and Fiona. Sadly she goes off to look for them. She is only young and she goes near the fishing boats. Two fishermen caught her. They didn't want her so they threw her onto the beach to die (because they are horrible to animals.) Some children came walking along the beach called Lucy and Thomas who are very nice to animals. They picked her up and are very surprised to see a sea horse on the beach. They ran home and put her in an old fish tank (which Sharon could fit in because she is only small.) They only kept her for a few hours then they let her go back to the ocean.

She swam back home. All her friends and family had looked all over for her and her dad was still looking for her. Everyone was so sad so she surprised them and they were happy again. She asked where they were before. They said they didn't really know, they just turned up in a dark sea which was all gloomy, then they heard a noise and they were back again but that's a different story.

Sharon started telling them about her adventure but she fell asleep. It was a long day.

Mariella Cardy (10)
Nenthead Primary School

A Day In The Life Of Donna

It was the Easter holidays and Gemma and her brother Justin were going swimming.

'I will beat you to the lake. I haven't been swimming in this lake before,' said Justin.
'I haven't either, I bet it is good.' But Gemma didn't know that a dolphin lived in there.

'What is that noise?' said Gemma.
'What noise?' said Justin. 'Oh no! I heard it. What is it? Wait there!' shouted Justin. 'I will see what it is.'
'Justin, be careful! What is it?'
'I don't know,' said Justin.

Gemma looked behind her and a big dolphin was there. 'Argh!' she screamed.
'What is it?' said Justin. 'Argh, now I know what you were screaming about. Let's go now.'
'Wait there! I don't think she will hurt us.'
'Yes, I think you're right. She will not hurt us. Shall we keep her as a pet?' said Gemma.
'Yes, that is a good idea. We'll play with her every day.'
'But what shall we call her?' asked Gemma.
'Donna,' suggested Justin.
'Yes, Donna the dolphin,' said Gemma. 'We will have to go for our dinner, we will play with her after.'

While they were having dinner they told their mum. After dinner they went to the lake and Donna was not there. They asked their mum, she didn't know where she was. They went to the beach and her dead body was getting carried by lots of men. Justin asked a man what had happened to the dolphin.

'Well, we moved her into the sea for a few minutes and she got attacked by a big shark.'

'Is she dead?' asked Gemma.

'Well yes,' said the man.

'We only played with her for a few minutes and now she is dead.'

From that day they were very unhappy and never went back to the lake again.

Samantha Bell (10)
Nenthead Primary School

A Day In The Life Of A Kitten

I am a new kitten. My mother is called Smudge and I am called Blacky because I am so black. I cuddle up to my mother every day when she's around. Sometimes she goes outside into the garden to play while me and my brothers and sisters play together. Well we usually fight. Oh I forgot to tell you, I have three brothers and sisters.

Whenever I try to walk I drag myself along with me because I am only three weeks and two days old and I haven't learnt to walk properly.

When I am six weeks old I might have to move to a different home because my owners cannot look after me, my mother and my three brothers and sisters.

At the moment I live behind the sofa because if I live anywhere else downstairs my mother moves us all. Me, my brothers and sisters cuddle up together when we go to sleep and when our mother is around.

I have now been sent to a lovely new home, with a lovely new owner and family. I have a lovely new playful friend called Toby. He is another cat and he is tabby and a year old.

Natalie Clifford (10)
Queens Road Primary School

A DAY IN THE LIFE OF A MOUTH

My name is Juicy, I am a mouth. People think it is always boring for me but it is not. Every single day of my life I get lots and lots of yummy, scrumptious and delicious food. It feels as though I am in heaven, especially with pizza, chips, chocolate and crisps. It's not just me who gets all the pleasure though, it's my friends too. Their names are Kanine, Molar and Incisors. They get the satisfaction of ripping, chewing and tearing the food.

Every day though, it is not just pleasure for me, it is also pain because I am opening and closing my mouth just so that I can talk. I don't want to but my owner makes me.

When my friends have had enough of munching the food, they get a really aching toothache. It is only about every 730 days though. It lasts 24 to 48 hours, sometimes it's longer but not often, and it's very rare.

Sometimes late at night I get very lonely so then I just try and sleep. As soon as I hit the pillow I do. Not all the time, but sometimes I need medicine before I go to sleep because I might have a toothache or something.

Rebecca Mills (11)
Queens Road Primary School

A DAY IN THE LIFE OF A HIKING BOOT

Hi, my name is Booty. I am a hiking boot and I ache all the time. My special features are a waterproof coating and a special design.

I am always on the go because my owner, John, is an excellent climber. Sometimes it is horrible because I get muddy and I hate it when I get muddy. Then again, I like it because I like the cold and wet dampness of the rocks meeting with my sole.

The best part is that Ropey (my best friend) comes with me all the time.

I am the one who protects John's feet and Ropey is the one who guides him on his way through the distance.

Oh yeah, I nearly forgot Rucky. Rucky is a rucksack and John puts all his gear in him, like Ropey of course.

Today we're going up a mountain called Mount Everest. Did you know that I know Mount Everest as well. He doesn't like being called that, he like sot be called Mounty (that's his nickname.)

Welcome back again and we're actually going on the walk now and 'I'm so excited and I just can't hide it. Come on, come on, come on because I want to, want to.' Ooops, sorry about that, I always get carried away and sing that song when we go on exciting walks like this.

I'll ring you back later, when we come off Mounty, Bye.

Amy Clow (10)
Queens Road Primary School

A DAY IN THE LIFE OF SEAWEED

I wake up to the sun glinting through the wavy water. As the sharks swim by on their early morning swim they sometimes murmur 'Hello' or 'Nice day.' As I lean here and there I speak to the starfish and chatter with the crabs as they scuttle past me busily. It's nearly time for the tide to go out and with this I go too.

I land on the beach, which is different from our peaceful world. I am surrounded by noisy children and people complaining about sand in their sandwiches. Then suddenly I'm picked up and put in a bucket with my friend Mr Crab and put in a rock pool; there I go to the reception, you see every rock pool is a seaweed (and other rock pool creatures) hotel. I am booked into room 9, but first I go and meet Mr Crab and Mrs Cockle, to talk and play kerpopel (a game rather like a human's game of chess but with three players and a giant board.) After that it was time for the tide to go out.

There I land back in my safe, peaceful home, well until the next tide and who knows that will happen then!

Rosie Smith (11)
Queens Road Primary School

A Day In The Life Of Stuart Little

Now, let me tell you about the day I turned into the fantastic Stuart Little. It was marvellous - with his cute little face and with his cute little whiskers. Also an excellent, amazing, fantastic car! If you would like to read more about this cool, little mouse with a cool, little car read on!

I was lying in my bed like a normal 11 year old kid, watching Stuart Little, when all of a sudden I turned into him. Mrs Little was shouting, 'Stuart, breakfast's ready.' Then I looked, I wasn't in my groovy chick bed. I was in a navy-blue king size bed and I was hairy. I was a mouse, I was Stuart Little.

I said tiredly, 'OK, OK, I'm coming.' I went downstairs. George and Mr and Mrs Little were eating their Kellogg's cornflakes. They took George to school. While they were away Snowbell came up to me and said, 'Hey, I'm the cat. It's my territory.'
Behind Snowbell was her friends that she could not see. They shouted, 'Ha ha, a cat playing with a mouse, it's the funniest thing we've ever seen.'

When Snowbell's friends went she said, 'Well, I'm not their friend now and I'm certainly not yours.' Mr and Mrs Little came back to give me my dinner. I had beans and sausage on toast with a bit of Victoria sponge - a lot for a mouse.

When Mr Little went to work, Mrs Little said happily to me, 'I will do the next load of washing then we will watch videos and play some of George's games.'
I replied, 'Thank you Mrs Little.' So we did exactly what Mrs Little said and it was brilliant.

Mr Little and George came home at 4.00pm and me and George went to play Monopoly in the attic for three hours. Mr and Mrs Little shouted up, 'Bedtime Stuart and George.' So we went to brush our teeth and then went to bed.

When I fell asleep I went round the world back to Carlisle and I opened my eyes and it was the end of the Stuart Little film and I was a normal 11 year old kid again!

Katie Spiers (11)
St Bede's RC Primary School, Carlisle

A Day In The Life Of Bart Simpson

Hi, I'm Matthew and I'm going to tell you about the time when I turned into Bart Simpson (off the Simpson's). It was absolutely amazing except for going to school. The one thing that really bugged me was having sisters (two). Now read on and you will find out what happened.

Right, I will start with Marge and Homer. Well, Homer was OK. He was always at Moes (pub). Marge, well all she did was whine about eating my vegetables, yuck! Then there was Maggie and Lisa, well all Lisa did was try to get me into trouble, she's just a goodie goodie all the time and then there was Maggie, well she was just a baby.

Now onto school, that was so boring! But it wasn't for Lisa, she loved it! I mean, anyone who loves school must be insane and get this, Maggie didn't even have to go to school or nursery. I mean, how unfair can you get? The teachers, well they were just normal, boring teachers. the best thing was about school was you got to meet Bart's friends, they were good fun. We always played footie. Now, I may not like football but would you say no to Bart's friends about playing footie? No, you wouldn't!

So did you enjoy the story. I hope you believe me because it really did happen, ask Bart. He had been in my world a day. So, *oh no, it's happening again. Ahh.*

Matthew Cully (11)
St Bede's RC Primary School, Carlisle

A Day In The Life Of Russell Crowe's Eyes

I got up in the morning in my lovely hotel suite in Germany; ready to film my new movie Gladiator.

I went downstairs for breakfast with all the other people involved in the film. Every single thing you could hope to eat was there, from packets of crisps to strawberry croissants. It was so nice.

Onto filming . . .

We went to the filming scene via helicopter, which was a bit snobbish when we could have just gone by coach.

The first scene was when we were fighting the Germans in Germany (or Germania, as they called it then.) The special effects were so magnificent that they could have been real!

We continued filming that one scene for the rest of the day until it was time to go back to the hotel. (It took us a long time to only remember five lines.) Tomorrow I think we'll do exactly the same, in my eyes.

Dominic Swift (11)
St Edward's Junior School, Liverpool

A Day In The Life Of Hercule Poirot

Today I had a case of a man named Roger Ackroyd who had connections with Edith Wright who had mysteriously died at exactly nineteen hundred hours on the 26th of May 1936.

Mr Ackroyd had invited me to his ultra-modern house which cost £500!

He was a charming man who had been brought up in an architect family. His daughter was also very formal and a gem to be with. So I accepted this lovely and charming invitation.

27th May 1936, Ackroyd's House

I walked into his house and his daughter, Estella, had the look of sheer terror on her face. 'What is bothering you my dear?' I asked.
'My . . . my father's been murdered!' stuttered Estella.
'Mmmm!' I muttered. I was thinking of a person who was evil and cold-hearted. I had no idea who it could be until I met a suspicious character along Moore Lane.

The person I met claimed to be called Mr Squeers. He had broad hips and a high-pitched tone just like a woman!

So I took him back to my house and gave him an interrogation session. *She* finally confessed she was a woman and did commit the murder! She was actually Mrs Wright. She also put a dummy of herself to make it look as though she had died!

I was disgusted. I sent her to court and she served her life in prison.

Judith Snape (11)
St Edward's Junior School, Liverpool

A Day In The Life Of Minnie Mouse

Today is a special day! Well, let's start from the morning. It went like this: I woke up at about 9.30am and got dressed into my *special* clothes because today I was going to be the *star* of the Disney Land Parade (with Mickey Mouse!) I got dressed in my special dress, which I only wear for *special* occasions! It is pink with white frills around the neck and along the bottom, it even has matching shoes and a bow to go in my hair! So anyway, at about 10.00am I was ready to go to the Disney Land parade.

Well, it was about 10.30 and I got loaded onto the float with my true love (the one and only) Mickey Mouse, hhhmmm. Anyway, back to life, it was about to start and I could hear the presenter welcoming us to the numerous amount of people who were waiting to see me! I couldn't believe it. The doors to the back of Disney had just opened. There I was, I had been waiting for this moment in time to happen for about *six* weeks! It felt breathtaking, but all I could do was smile. I could see the finishing gate where we go to finish off the parade, so I thought I would give it my very, very best.

Shortly after the finish and all the autographs etc, we were all allowed to go home thinking hopefully we would get asked back next year.

Juliet Falconer (10)
St Edward's Junior School, Liverpool

A Day In The Life Of A Teacher

Mr Jones wakes up every week day and goes to school. He sits in the staff room for a while and then goes to his classroom. 'Right class, all sit down and pay attention. Today we are going to learn about planets. First off, James name me two planets.'

'Earth and Jupiter sir.'

'Very good James. Kate can you name me two planets?'

'Mars and Pluto sir.'

'Very good Kate. Right class, I want you to all write a paragraph about as many planets as you can think of. That should last you all until break time.'

After break - 'Right class, maths books out. So children, welcome to the lovely world of maths, ha ha ha. You will like this lesson, it's a written test. I will hand out a booklet to each of you. James, pass them around please. You will have fifteen minutes to finish starting from now.'

Fifteen minutes later - 'Right class, pens and paper down and line up, music with Mrs Bixter.'

'Attention class Y5J, let's sing this song called Little Light Of Mine, it's on page 20. A one, a two, a one two three four. This little light of mine, I'm going to let it shine on you, my love, yeah, yeah.'

Later in the day - 'Class, it's time for the last lesson of the day. Put away all library books and quietly head back to our classroom for art. What I would like you to do is draw a picture in a pattern then colour it in. Remember children, I want some nice pictures to hang on walls.'

It's home time now and Mr Johnson is tired. He had a lovely day today and I can't wait for tomorrow.

James Johnson (9)
St Edward's Junior School, Liverpool

A Day In The Life Of Me

My name is Kate and I go to St Edward's Junior School. It was in the summer term that me and my friends Helen, Clare and Sophie got very bored. It was raining. It had rained hard for the past eight weeks. Sports training was cancelled because of the rain. We couldn't play out because of the rain. During the geography lesson the following afternoon us four went down to the cellar for a drink. When we got to the bottom of the cellar stairs we saw a door we had never seen before. Helen cautiously opened it and we followed her through.

Our first view of the room gave us all quite a shock. It was filled with dead bodies, the ghosts that had evolved from the bodies, and pools of blood. We stood still, unable to move a muscle. Then one of the ghosts spoke up. 'You must kill the basilik like it killed us. Once you have done that take the key that we all desire bring it back and we will all be free. You will find him by going back through the door in which you came, you will find yourselves in a long corridor, the basilik lives at the other end.'

As we got to the sleeping basilik we picked up the sword lying next to it and stuck it into the basilik's heart. The basilik gave a yelp of pain and started to chase us. We ran, I was clutching the key, then the basilik grabbed hold of Clare's leg but luckily Sophie was able to free it. I ran to the door and turned the key into the lock, suddenly we were back in the cellar, the basilik had gone. The ghosts had gone, everything had disappeared. The only thing remaining was a speck of blood on Helen's coat.

When we got home we didn't tell anyone what had happened. They would never believe us if we did.

Kate Biltcliffe (10)
St Edward's Junior School, Liverpool

A Day In The Life Of A Fairy

My name is Bluebell and my day begins washing my beautiful, glittery pink wings and putting on my new dress which I made with red rose petals and spider's silk that my pet Webster made for me. I have my breakfast of dew, from the tall grass outside my tree hole, and honey which my pet Bumble collected for me. Now I'm off to work as the King's messenger. But first I have to report to the King to find out where I have to go. Here I am at the King's palace. Oh isn't it beautiful and isn't it a good place to start my day?

'Excuse me, but where is the King?' I say.
'Well you see, the King went out for his morning ride on his pet dragonfly and never came back. We don't know what to do,' replies the adviser.
'I think you should put on a search party to find him.'
'Will that work?' asks the adviser.
'I don't know, but we should try.' Now I'm off to search for the King with the advisers.

'Watch out for the beehive! Look, there's the King's dragonfly. Come on, let's go.'
'I'm not going down there. The last time I went near that thing it bit me. Do you want to see the scar?' says the chief adviser.
'Fine, you don't have to go down there, but I am and the rest of us are, so you will be on your own.'
'Fine, I'll come down, but if I get bitten I'm blaming it on you,' he says at last.
'Fine! Do you know where the King is?' I ask the dragonfly.
'Let's face it, the dragonfly can't talk,' says one of the advisers.
'No, you're wrong there because I have some magic dust which will make him talk,' I say.
'Where did you get that?' asks one of the advisers.
'Oh, I picked it up at the palace.'
'Oh right, good.'

As soon as the magic dust hits the dragonfly he starts to talk. 'Yes, I do know where the King is,' the dragonfly says.
'Could you please tell us?'

'The King was captured by an ugly centipede and taken to his hole to be eaten for dinner,' the dragonfly said.

'Do you know where the centipede's hole is?'

'Yes I do. His hole is right by the old man's pond.'

'Come on, we have to go to save the King.'

It hasn't taken us long to get to the pond, but even as we arrive I can see that the centipede is already setting up his barbecue. While some of the advisers stay and watch the centipede, I sneak around to the cage where the King is being kept and quietly open the door. The King stretches his wings, gives a couple of flaps and we are off back to the palace before the centipede realises that the King has been rescued.

Emily Simpson (10)
St Edward's Junior School, Liverpool

A Day In The Life Of A Surf Dude

I am one of those people who hang around on the beach all day waiting for the perfect wave. People call me a surf dude. I live in a tent on the beach in Fuerteventura in the Canary Islands. Lots of people live like me. I usually wake up late, after a night of lots of partying by the campfire with all my friends. My dog sleeps, eats and surfs with me. When we wake up the first thing we do is make a cup of tea on the leftover heat of the campfire, then my dog, Sally, and I go for a walk down to the sea for a wash.

I watch the sea and the clouds to get an idea of what the weather will be like today. Today is good because the surf is up and the weather is just right. I go back for my breakfast which is a huge bacon butty today and some coffee. After my breakfast I get out my board and check it for any scrapes from yesterday's surfing. My board looks good so I head off to my favourite part of the beach where I said I will meet all my friends.

When I get there they are ready and waiting for me, as usual I am the last to get up. Very soon we are laying on our boards paddling hard to get out past all the breakers to the big, green waves, this is extremely hard work so when we get there we just lie on our backs on our boards and float up and down on the swell while we get our breath back.

Soon we are ready to go. I can see Sally my dog sniffing around in the rock pools waiting for me. I am looking behind me until I see the best wave then I start swimming. As I feel the wave picking up I get onto my knees, then jump onto my feet. I lean forwards and shift my feet until my balance is just right. I am now heading very fast towards the beach, it is exhilarating. I can feel the speed and the spray hitting my face, it takes all my concentration to keep up.

I do this all day, resting now and again lying in the hot sun on the beach. Eventually we head back to the tents and eat fish on the barbecue. I lie back with Sally on my lap and watch the sun go down.

Life is good.

Tristen Meacham-Day (10)
St Edward's Junior School, Liverpool

A DAY IN THE LIFE OF MY CAT

Hello! My name is Oscar the cat. I live with five owners, Charlotte, Jonathan, Isobel, Anne and Dennis. I am a brown, toffee-white and grey colour with long fur. I have two close friends called Monster and Perkins. Today, my owners have just left on their holidays and have forgotten to leave me any food!

I suppose I'll have to get it by myself. Good job I'm a clever cat. I'll go and look in Charlotte's friend's house. If I climb the wall I'll be able to see if there are any fish in the pond. Yes! There are, here comes dinner! Splash! Oh no, I've fallen in; I hate water and no fish either.

Perhaps the fish and chip shop might be the place. My owners often go there, hmmm! I can smell the cod, lovely. Woof! Woof! The chip shop owner has a large Alsatian and I might end up as his dinner. I'd better leave.

It's a lovely day so I'll try the park for some birds. Yummy! Some duck! Ouch! That one tried to nip me, better look for something smaller. I think I'll go home, looking for food is tiring. I'll just try the back of the house where my cat flap is. Oh look, Dennis's mum's car is outside. I'll go round the back. *Hooray!* She's left me some dinner, they didn't forget me after all. It's a long day when you are a hungry cat so I think I'll settle down for a good sleep and as they are still away I can sleep on the bed.

Purr . . . fect!

Charlotte Cattrall (9)
St Edward's Junior School, Liverpool

A DAY IN THE LIFE OF QUEEN ELIZABETH II

Dear diary, it's just another one of those days. I've been on the go all day. Nobody knows how hard it is to be Queen. I mean, I know it sounds great having an extremely large mansion, but really you can't come out of it without being photographed.

I came out to get into the limousine and as usual I was photographed, of course, giving a very large smile and my tedious royal wave. I was on my way to open the new department of St Edward's Junior School, Runnymede. I was wearing my new and stylish turquoise-blue suit with matching hat, gloves, bag and shoes. When I got to St Edward's, I found the children very polite and helpful. The new department was very nice and the computer suite was very high tech.

In the opening ceremony some children played instruments and sang. There was brass, recorder, guitar, speech choir and choir. At the end, Mr Sweeney (the headmaster) handed me the scissors so I could cut the ribbon and open the new department. In my speech, I hoped that the children would enjoy learning and use their skills to make my kingdom a better place. After that, Mr Sweeney offered me some refreshments and then I went home to put my feet up. Then after my little nap I got changed into my aqua-marine suit to have dinner with the rest of my family.

I was walking to the dining room, when suddenly I fell down a trapdoor and landed head first. I hurt my head so badly, that I fainted. When I woke up, I saw a misty figure floating above me. I couldn't quite make out who it was but when she spoke I knew it was Queen Victoria. 'Hello Victoria, I haven't seen you in a while,' I said.
'Be quiet! I want you to find the coin with my face on and give it to me by midnight or I will kill you!' she said.

I had to say I'd try because I had a fifty-fifty chance of staying alive!

Queen Victoria gave me a ladder to climb back up to the palace hall. Never in my royal life had I been so scared. I checked the dressing room first, but I couldn't find it. I had checked half the palace by 6.00pm, but no luck. I went to my bedroom to find a clip for my hair because it was getting in my way. I took the clip out when suddenly the jewellery box spat out the coin. I grabbed it and made a run for the palace hall. Again I fell down the passage, but this time I didn't faint Queen Victoria was floating in mid-air with a big smile on her face. I gave her the coin which was of great value to her. I had succeeded in my task, and that was the end of a very eventful day in the life of Queen Elizabeth II.

Clare O'Brien (9)
St Edward's Junior School, Liverpool

A Day In The Life Of A Cameraman

I woke up on the plane journey. Slowly I got up with the racing scarlet skies. The news crew . . . dead, or so it seemed. No, only asleep. The plane landed with a jerk. The news crew stood up slothfully and walked out the plane like drones. I followed with only my camera and rucksack. As the sun dawned on Israel, I noticed serene peace, soon to be shattered by gunshots and violence.

Beer bottles, shotgun pellets and cigarettes lay scattered on the street. We reached one of the prime spots of the war, the noise gathering like a swarm of bees. Swiftly we strapped on our bullet-proof vests and were ready to roll. The takes seemed to multiply like rabbits. The noise was too intense, we had to put our earplugs in. We heard an explosion. A gust of wind and dust came shooting into our faces and stung our eyes savagely.

The attacks were getting even more brutal and buildings were getting set on fire and some children were getting murdered but I could not stop it. I am Rapunzel with no prince. Helpless on an island. People are shooting each other but all I can do is shoot the news.

Aaron Morrison-Griffiths (10)
St Edward's Junior School, Liverpool

A DAY IN THE LIFE OF A SHOPPING TROLLEY

I'm waiting outside Tesco for someone to use me. I spot a family heading towards me. They wheel me off into the supermarket towards the freezers. The mum pops some chicken nuggets, fish fingers and chips into me for the children. Then the mum pops a frozen chicken inside and wheels me round the corner to the drinks section. The dad goes to get his beer while the children start dumping cola and fizzy orange into me.

Next they push me straight ahead to get crisps, baked beans, bread, cornflakes and porridge. While the mum and children are choosing sweets, the dad pops the beer and wine in me.

Next we go round the corner and pick up a bag of potatoes. The children put fruit into the trolley; in go the bananas and oranges. The dad starts dumping carrots, sprouts, cabbages and peppers. The mum goes to the freezer to get some semi-skimmed milk. The children go back to the freezers to get some ice cream. The dad goes to get some washing powder and washing-up liquid. Then it's off to the till. The bill is £69.00. Mum gets out her Visa card to pay. Then it's off to the trolley stand for me for the next customer.

Robert Hall (11)
St John's CE Primary School, Crossens

A Day In The Life Of Anne Frank

23rd September 1941

06.45 - Hello Kitty, I've just woken up and I am looking out of the window. It is all steamed up but I think I can see people running around scared, in the street below, which is normally a sign that the Nazis are coming.

Father is going to start school lessons with us today. I can't wait but Margot doesn't want to.

09.30 - Father did the first lessons after breakfast. When mother finally woke up, it was English. We started doing describing words and then we had to describe how we felt about staying in hiding for so long . . .

14.40 - I can see, down there on the ground below, I can hear windows being smashed and I can smell smoke. I can see flames creeping down the road reaching out to all that are Jewish or are different from Nazis. But what's that? The flames have stopped! Some people have put the fire out! Oh no! I can hear more people screaming now. The Nazis are coming. I can hear them, I can see them, I feel like I can smell them.

I'm so angry. How dare they do that! But I have sat here every day, I have lived in his attic, but what can I do? I am just a poor little Jewish girl.

17.20 - The Nazis have now gone and they missed us, that was another thing we narrowly escaped.

Frankie Stubbs (11)
St John's CE Primary School, Crossens

A Day In The Life Of Child's Favourite Teddy

My paw has just been grabbed, now for the bumpy trip downstairs. Why does Louise always have to bang my head on the stairs?

I'm so fed up with this every day. Can't there be something more exciting to do? Sat propped against the fruit bowl. What's that wet feeling creeping up my leg? Oh no, Louise has spilt her breakfast all over me!

'Dusty, your bear will have to go into the wash,' I heard Louise's mum say. I was put on top of a very smelly T-shirt and some socks. I stayed there for about an hour. I've never been in the washer before. As I was wondering what it would be like, someone threw me in the washer. Some soapy water came rushing out from a hole behind me. Suddenly I started spinning around.

At last I stopped after twenty minutes but it felt more like a year. I turned my head only to see Louise's mum's hand coming for me. My ear was pegged to the line. Sopping wet, uncomfortable, longing to be hugged, I hung. Swaying gently in the breeze I hung for what seemed like hours. Louise's older sister took me down.

As soon as I got in, Louise hugged me and I was dragged up the stairs - bump, bump and into bed. I never want to have to do anything different again, that's for sure!

Mikaela Clarke (10)
St John's CE Primary School, Crossens

A DAY IN THE LIFE OF A TEN PENCE COIN

Crash! There I go, from an elderly man's pocket into the till. I lie there amongst all the other identical ten pence coins, waiting for the cash register to open again.

Rattle, rattle, rattle. The lady behind the counter picks up twenty pences, two pences, fifty pences and a one pound coin. Every other coin apart from me, the lonely ten pence, wait . . . rattle. 'It's me, it's me!' I shout.

'One pound and sixty-two pence change,' says the lady as the young gentleman stuffs me in the back pocket of his jeans. Where to next?
'Ouch, you're sitting on me!' I said, quite muffled.
'Brummm,' revved the engine of the young man's car.

The man got out of his car and must not have heard the clang of me, falling on the pavement outside his house. There I sat watching cars whiz past me for about an hour!

'Hey, get your grubby mitts off me!' I shouted. A little girl had just picked me up with her dirty hands and put me in her top pocket.
'Off to the shop then!' says her father. 'I'll buy your sweets.' Phew, I was safe. When we got to the girl's house, she put me in her piggy bank.

With all of the chaos today, goodness knows what tomorrow will bring!

Lauren Stirk (10)
St John's CE Primary School, Crossens

A Day In The Life Of A Classroom Chair

I got woken up by all the children, the noisy lot, then I got squashed again by Phillip. Phillip's in a mood. I can tell because he's slamming his books down and stomping around.

'Ooh,' cried the table, 'that hurt!'
'Ohh,' cried the floor, 'that hurt!'

At last all the children have gone to lunch, they really are a horrible bunch. I thought that I could relax and rest, but Mrs Caff sat on me and made me feel sick. My legs are aching so much.

'Arrhh!' I cried, 'my legs are broken.'

I was crying, I am in so much pain, but the funny thing was Mrs Caff fell off the chair. Mrs Caff got up and went to get Mr Fillgo, the maths teacher. Mr Fillgo's name was Mike.

'Err Mike, have you got a minute?' asked Mrs Caff.
'Yes, why?' replied Mike.
'Well the chair is broken and I was wondering if you could fix it,' explained Mrs Caff.
'Well, OK.'

Mrs Caff and Mr Fillgo came into the classroom. Mr Fillgo fixed me up. I felt much better.

When all the children came in after lunch Mrs Caff told them all about me and I felt very proud.

It's now 6.00pm. All the teachers have just gone home. I relaxed and rested. I fell asleep thinking about what will happen tomorrow.

Amy Down (10)
St Mary's CE Primary School, Eastham

A DAY IN THE LIFE OF A DOG

Teddy, the dog, got up early on Saturday morning and came into all of our bedrooms. He licked all of our faces. When we got up Teddy was ready for his breakfast so Debbie went and gave him his breakfast. Debbie, Wesley and Gemma went to have a wash and to get dressed. As we went to make the beds we didn't know that Teddy was behind us and when we had finished, Teddy jumped onto it. Debbie had to make the bed again. Then we all went to do our teeth and started to drink the water from the sink.

Five o'clock came and Teddy was thinking he was hungry and wanted his tea, so we had tea at six o'clock. Teddy gobbled his down and then wanted to have a mad half hour. When Debbie, Wesley and Gemma had finished their tea, they let Teddy have his mad half hour which lasted until eight o'clock. Debbie then said, 'It's time to stop.'

Debbie, Wesley, Gemma and Teddy had some supper, watched some TV, then they all went to bed. At first Teddy slept on Debbie's bed, then he went to sleep at the top of the stairs. They all went to sleep, suddenly Teddy heard a noise and ran down the stairs and barked, so Gemma went to wake her mum up and she said, 'It's only Teddy.'

Gemma Bayley (10)
St Mary's CE Primary School, Eastham

A DAY IN THE LIFE OF DAVID BECKHAM

I wake up and go to the bathroom to get washed and dressed. When that's done I go and make a start on the breakfast. We are having bacon, egg and fried bread. It is Saturday so I have football. We are going to the Dell. We are having a match against Southampton. We have two hours training. Today we are practising volleys and Fabian Barthez is saving shots.

We had kick-off. Already a very good shot was saved. 'Unlucky Andy,' I said. I've got the ball, I'm running into the penalty area, I shoot, I score! There are two minutes left until full-time. I'm taking Andy Cole and Ryan Giggs home.

We arrived home at 7.09pm. I was extremely tired so I'm having an early night. I went to bed at 10.30pm and I'll have a lie-in in the morning.

Christopher Brown (10)
St Mary's CE Primary School, Eastham

A DAY IN THE LIFE OF A TEACHER

This morning I was woken up by the thought of marking tests. I ate my breakfast whilst marking the tests and I spilt some milk on them.

I arrived at school very late and the kids are having fun. I went in and they all sat down. They've been naughty so I'll give them a spelling test to get my own back on them, I thought.

All the children sat on the carpet raring to go and work. I surprised them by saying, 'This morning we will have a nice, friendly spelling test to start the day.' I heard a mixture of yes and no.

'I am still mad at you so to cheer me up we will have a maths test.' All the children thought it was a good idea, so I made it hard.

I sat down and ate my lunch thinking tests, tests. I enjoyed my lunch but I didn't want to go back and work. The children wanted to go and play football on the field. I said, 'No, we will have a science test about electricity.'

History was fun, but I lost my voice because of shouting. 'We will now draw a picture of Queen Victoria,' I tried to say, 'here is a picture of her to copy from.'

By home time my voice had come back. We all said our prayer and said good afternoon.

'Tomorrow bring your favourite book and an A4 page of why you like it,' I said.

Everyone, apart from me, had gone home. I sat down and marked the tests and commented on the pictures. I thought, I wish I didn't do these tests.

'It is half past five and I want to go home, but I've got to think of some more tests,' I said to myself.

Finally I was able to go home. 'Yes!' I went home with a smile on my face and with no books to mark.

At half past seven I settled down and had my tea. Mmm, that was delicious, I said after finishing it all. I put my dressing gown and went to bed.

Jenny Davies (11)
St Mary's CE Primary School, Eastham

A DAY IN THE LIFE OF MY BROTHER

'Why do I have to get up so late, I'll have no time to go out if I'm not quick,' whispers Dan.
'At last, there's your breakfast. You'll have to put it in the microwave to warm it up,' says Mum.
'Whatever!' says Dan.
'Hi,' says George.
'Mum, I've got washed and dressed but I'm still doing my hair!'
'OK! I don't know, you spend more time with your hair than you do with your family,' mumbles Mum.
'Dan, do you want to play footie in the front,' asked George.
'After yeah, I'm going out now,' he replies grumpily.
'Dad, can you give me a lift to Cheshire Oaks at 1.00pm?'
'Yeah!'

Dan goes onto the computer, loads up Napster and puts Eminem on, shuts the door and goes onto the Internet. His dad takes both Ray and Dan out.

Ring, ring, ring, ring, ring.

'Hello, is Mum or Dad there George,' says Dan.
'Yeah!'
'Well can you get one of them for me?' says Dan.
'OK,' replied George.

Dan got picked up and they played football in the front.

'Dan, George, tea,' shouts Mum.
'I've already had tea at McDonald's,' says Dan.
'All the more for you Dad then.'

They all have their showers and watch television whilst Dan goes on the computer and downloads some music.

By 11.00pm Mum is asleep on the settee and Dan, George and their dad are watching Match of the Day. Their dad promised them that they could go to Plymyard Fields for a game of football or basketball tomorrow. After Goal of the Month on Match of the Day they decided to go to bed.

'I'll just put my phone on charge,' whispers Dan.

Georgina Corner (10)
St Mary's CE Primary School, Eastham

A DAY IN THE LIFE OF SERGEI REBROV

I am Sergei Rebrov. I usually wake up at six o'clock to get ready for a match. I have my breakfast then wash and finally get dressed.

At seven-thirty I start my journey to London ready to play Villa. On the way I pick up some of my team mates.

I get to London at eleven o'clock and then I have to find the ground of White Hart Lane. Eleven-thirty, I find the ground. We all go in and discuss our team tactics for the big match. All of my team start training.

At 13.00 - the match starts between Tottenham and Aston Villa. The first goal is scored by me and I am running as fast as I can. At 13.45pm I start shooting. The half-time whistle went with the score 1-0 to Spurs thanks to me.

Ben Silas (10)
St Mary's CE Primary School, Eastham

A DAY IN THE LIFE OF A TEACHER

I got up at 6.30am. I had breakfast. I got dressed, got in my car and went to school. When I got there I sorted my things out. By the time I had finished the children had come in. I said to them, 'Line up,' but Sarah and Charlotte were talking, so I told them to stop.

While they were in assembly, I put their work on the board. When the kids came back in I did the registration. Jenny wasn't in.

The first thing I did with the children was maths. The children were doing times tables.
'What times tables are we doing today?' asked Becky.
They are doing their 11 times tables. The children worked on them until 10.30am, because then it was playtime. When it was playtime I played football with some of them.

We went in at 10.40am. I told the children to finish their work and then sit in their seats, because they were going to do English.

In English they did a spelling test, a really big one. I thought that all of them would do quite well.

Next I read until lunch. I told the children to go to lunch. While I did my marking I had my lunch.

Amy asked in the playground if we could play rounders, so we played rounders.

After dinner was PE. The children had a good game of tennis.
'Go in and get changed. When you are changed sit in your seats, we're going to do science about mould on bread.'

It was nearly home time. After the children had gone home I stayed until 8.00pm to mark, then I went home, watched TV and went to bed.

Katie Chetta (11)
St Mary's CE Primary School, Eastham

A Day In The Life Of Robbie Williams

I get out of bed, order the maid to make me a champagne breakfast and I have lots of toast. I get into the hot tub, order the maid to get my best outfit. I watch TV on my two wall TV.

I get in my limousine, order Joe the chauffeur to go to the studios, do some singing, work on my new Pepsi advertisement.

I go to a friend's home, Geri, and arrange to go clubbing. We have a chat, then I go home.

I have a good play with the dog. I get ready to meet Geri. We have a good night.

James Lewis (10)
St Mary's CE Primary School, Eastham

A Day In The Life Of A Wild Tiger

Aaahhh, I needed that stretch. It's very bright outside.

I creep through the long, dry grass. It really tickles. Doh, there is a pack of wild oxen. The last one I tasted was lovely, the meat was really tender and juicy. I hope I can catch another one like that.

Here I go. Whoah! These oxen can run very, very fast. I think I'll go for a mum which has a baby. The baby won't last long without its mum.

Yes! I got one! Now all I have to do is find a quiet spot where there are no vultures. Last time vultures came and ate quite a bit of my meal.

Boy, this is heavy. Aahh. This looks like a nice spot to eat. Ummm. How gorgeous is this? It is just as nice as the one yesterday. I really am tired. I think I will go to that tree over there and lie down.

I can't believe how long I slept. I knew I was tired but I didn't think I was *that* tired. After that sleep I'm really hungry. I shall go hunting for a baby buffalo.

I think I shall try by the water-hole. Ah, there's one now.

Huh. There's something behind me. Oh no, it's a . . . cobra. I have to run.

Phew! I'm glad I'm safe. Yum. There's the buffalo. Gotcha. Now I'll take it back to the den. What a catch.

Oh, there's Jake. 'Oi Jake, I'm coming to get you.'
'Hi Stripe, you won't if I can help it.'

Phew, I'm really tired. 'Oh hi again Jake.'
'Are you going home?'
'Yes.'
Here's my den. 'Night.'
'Night.'

Sarah Rainford (10)
St Mary's CE Primary School, Eastham

A DAY IN THE LIFE OF A DOG

I woke up and gave my owner a sign to tell him to take me out for business, so he woke up and took me out into the garden. I could tell that my owner wasn't very happy for waking him up this early, so I played a growling game with him and as always I won. His growl was like a bear but my growl was like a lion.

After a while my owner's mum saw me lying down and knew I was bored, so she taught me to roll over, give us ya paw, sit, lie down and jump all at the same time. As I was on the floor I could hear someone speaking, the voice was familiar, but too far away. When it started coming closer and closer I realised it was my owner. I jumped up and ran outside with joy and licked him all over.

Before bedtime I watched an animal channel and didn't know what type of language it was speaking, so I just kept on walking up to the speakers.

Craig Hughes (10)
St Mary's CE Primary School, Eastham

A DAY IN THE LIFE OF HUW EDWARDS

I wake up and then, in a rush, have a very quick breakfast. The next feature of my day is getting to Television Centre. I normally get a taxi or tube there.

I'm firstly welcomed in by the producer; then I go to the internet suite and look for the latest news on the website.

After that, I put all the news stories in order of what matters to the viewers. There's normally a lot of people talking, so it is a very irritating time for me.

By now I'm often very tired, so I have lunch, but the time sails by and before I know where I am, I'm trying to pronounce names like Muttian Muralitharan and places like Azerbayan. Sometimes you do get fed up!

Now it's time for the make-up, it seems everything is being slapped on my face! A mirror is then thrust in front of me so I can see myself.

There is only an hour to go so I rush to my desk and do link-up rehearsals with all the reporters. Finally I have some more of my lines to go over. The nerves set in a fair bit.

I'm now ready to present the news.

The first 15 minutes are normally fine, but there are difficulties half way through the programme because I have to either say 'It's quarter past 6, or 'It's 15 minutes past 6.'

I then introduce the weather presenter, followed by me saying, 'I'll be back at 7, bye for now.'

Daniel Tyler (11)
St Mary's CE Primary School, Eastham

A DAY IN THE LIFE OF AN ALIEN

Zoggo woke up and yawned. He lived with his mum and dad on Kloggle, a planet belonging to the first star of Orion's Belt. He climbed out of his concrete sheets and went to the next town for breakfast.

'Hello Mum, hello Dad, how terrifyingly ugly you both look this morning!' he exclaimed, sitting down to his slugs in salt and Pog-poo.
'So, Zoggo,' Mum began, 'where do you want to live today then?'
'I think I'll go to Earth,' he replied as he jumped out of the toilet bowl, into his Space-o five hundred and started the engine.

His fuel gauge said he had fifty gallons of apple juice left. So he said goodbye to the native Plobbies and sped off for Earth.

When he finally reached his destination, he found a strange building with lots of little Earthlings in. 'What a very peculiar place to imprison those ugly-looking creatures. I think I heard Mum say they were called school children, funny things an' all, too.' Zoggo whispered to himself.

He walked into a classroom where some school children were pestering a teacher. Zoggo went outside into the corridor by the packed lunches and opened one with the words *Fay Hurley* on it. Inside the box there was a carton of apple juice. He stole it and leapt into his spaceship.

His five hour journey took him back to Kloggle where he climbed into bed and dreamed about his day.

Kristina Hurley (10)
South Walney Junior School

A DAY IN THE LIFE OF ME

I get up in the morning and say to myself, 'Here we go.' I walk through the school gates and feel as if everyone is staring at me. Usually I stand by my friends and talk to them, but for some reason they wouldn't speak. I just carried on walking, feeling hurt and alone. When I get in the classroom I feel even worse because I have to sit next to a popular boy who is always making fun of me. I want to cry but I can't breathe, he would make fun of me even more. At dinner time I don't feel too bad because sometimes somebody says hello.

At play time I go and talk to the midday assistants, at least they talk back. Then all of a sudden Chantelle, the most popular girl in the school comes up to me and says, 'Do you want to play?'
I was stuck for words. 'Yes.' So I go and play.

Later that day Dave starts speaking to me, he wasn't insulting or criticising me, he was being nice for a change. So the day carried on like that.

When I got home I felt happy and glad, but I still felt upset about my friends ignoring me. So, being brave, I picked up the phone and dialled one of my friends' numbers. Melissa answered the phone, we started talking and crying, but we made friends.

That's my life.

Zoe Humphrey (11)
Stanney Grange CP School

A DAY AT MY CARAVAN

One day there was a caravan site in Towyn and my mum and dad thought it would be a good idea to buy a caravan, so we did. The day that we bought it we went into town and we bought some things for the caravan.

After we decorated the caravan we went out to the Welsh mountain zoo and we saw all the wonderful animals and all the many different reptiles. When we came out of the Welsh mountain zoo we went to the arcades and I spent some money. I spent about £2 and I won the jackpot twice, so we all went to McDonald's and we had something to eat.

Then, when we were finished in McDonald's we went to the sun centre and went on the big slides and I went into the swimming pool. When we came out of the swimming bathes, it was time to go home but my mum said that before we go home, we could go to the cinema. So we went into the cinema and we watched Star Wars Episode One. It was about two people who had powers of the unnatural who had to destroy an evil force, but one died. Then we came out of the cinema and went home and that was my day at my caravan.

Graham Huckle (11)
Stanney Grange CP School

A Day In The Life Of The Mayor

One cold night, I was sitting by my window when a shooting star shot past, so I decided to make a wish. 'I wish I could be the Mayor for one day.' A stupid wish, it won't come true anyway.

'Come on Mr Mayor, time to get up.'

'What time is it?'

'It's six o'clock, Mr Mayor.'

'Wait, you just called me Mr Mayor.'

'You are the Mayor.'

'I'm the Mayor?'

'Yes Sir, you are.'

'I'm the Mayor! Yes, my wish came true.' So that morning I spent one hour playing tennis, it was spectacular.

'Come on Sir, you've got a conference.'

'So Mr Mayor, what do you think we should do about the children's attitude in school?'

'Some of their lessons are boring, so let them pick the first lesson.'

'Brilliant Mr Mayor!'

Once I got back I played golf for the very first time. I like being the Mayor so far. I have three hundred pounds, I can have anything I want, it's great! I want to be the Mayor forever; it's easy being the Mayor, I can do it no problem. Ding-dong, it's twelve o'clock! It's time to be a child again, well it was great while it lasted.

Simon Randall (11)
Stanney Grange CP School

A DAY IN THE LIFE OF ...

It was Friday in Egypt and there was a girl and her mother, they were walking to the River Nile to get some water. The girl's mother, Taraisa, hit the girl for no reason at all, 'Stop it Talolla,' shouted Taraisa. Then they stopped.

'What did you do that for?' said Talolla, then she jumped into the river. Then she realised that she could breathe underwater. Talolla could talk to the fish, she was having a wonderful time with them. Then a wonderful thing happened, her legs turned into a mermaid's tail. She was amazed, then she found herself swimming in the coral reef. Then she saw a shark come up to her as if it was going to eat her. 'Are you going to eat me?' said worried Talolla. But she was shocked, it was not a normal shark, it was a kind shark looking for her baby. So they could set off again.

'Here he is,' said the shark.

'Oh, have you found him?' asked worried Talolla.

'Yes,' shouted the shark. 'I will have to go home now.'

Talolla found herself back in the River Nile and she lived happily ever after in the river.

Natalie Blundell (10)
Stanney Grange CP School

A DAY IN THE LIFE OF A FOOTBALL

It all started one morning in JJB Sport . . . the door opened and a boy walked towards me, and picked up the football next to me. *Phew!* He bounced it, put it back, picked me up and carried me to the counter! Then he kicked me all the way to the car.

I was at the place humans call home. The boy dribbled me into the garden. I could see another boy who seemed to be coming closer and closer. Then *oooofffff* he's getting further and further - I think I was being kicked! I was told it hurt, but this was like flying! Then I went closer and closer and further and further and further but not closer to the boy. Then *aaahhhh, ow!* I had hit the ground. The next thing I heard was cheering, then a whistle went. 'Free kick.' *Bam.* Suddenly I was being chased by twenty-two men in different colours. I had never been faster in my life. I didn't even notice the pain of being kicked by forty-four studded feet from one end of the pitch to another.

I had been kicked around for ages. *Aaaaahhh* I'm in the net. The referee blows his whistle again, end of match. I'm being picked up and carried into a room and signed by players. Wait, there's my owner! I bet he's glad I've been signed. Not half as glad as I am to see him again!

John Forster (10)
Sunnymede School

A Day In The Life Of A Jaguar

The sun was beating down through the luscious leaves. I opened my eyes and I saw a boar. It had big, long, sharp tusks. I stood up and I was after him, I caught him. It was quite easy to catch him. I ripped some meat off him and it was delicious. Once I got most of the meat off him, some mean vultures came down and ate the scraps. I walked over to a big, hollow log and I came to a rock. I had a nap.

As I woke I was hungry again, so I crawled through the long, dead grass. Then I pounced and the chase was on. I ran after the smallest antelope and I came to the side of it and I jumped, and with my vicious, sharp, puncturing teeth I tore some of the skin off the antelope. Sitting down I stuck my sharp jaws into the flesh. It was great. The taste was magnificent, scrumptious even.

Just as I was half way through my lunch, an adult antelope ran at me like a bull and it punctured me with its sharp horns. The pain was stunning. I limped off the savannah ground and I limped into the forest. It was still hurting but I was going to survive. What a pity I couldn't finish my mouth-watering lunch of an antelope. Maybe next time.

Andrew Gartside (10)
Sunnymede School

A Day In The Life Of Jumbo, The Car

Click. The key opens my shiny, white front door. Something light, like a leaf in the wind, and something heavy are put in. Ah! I'm woken ten minutes later. Angry, I start an extravagant stall.

Well, I started. Eventually! Now I'm sitting on my 'black as coal tyres'. Hang on, where are we going now? The destination; the petrol station. We're here. Lovely! The icy cold drink of slimy, delicious petrol slipped through me with ease.

Then we're off to a huge building with enormous green letters on it. Of course! This is where the pink people who drive me get their food.

Zzzeerrr.
'Volvo.'
'What?'
'Here. It's the silver BMW next to you.'
'What do you want?' I asked bewildered.
'A chat,' said the BMW.
I could see he was built for aerodynamics and speed. He boasted about his life on the fast motorways of England.

The wind was howling in my drive. It was like the blistering conditions of the Arctic to a car like me. But I had had a wonderful chat with the BMW - even if he was a bit of a know-it-all. The last trip of the day soon, to pick up more funny pink people.

I was just about to sleep when, *bang!* 'Ouch.' A tile slid off the roof right into the middle of my bonnet in the middle of the night. It's given me a nasty dent.

The end to an exciting, enjoyable, interesting day!

Oliver Guest (10)
Sunnymede School

A DAY IN THE LIFE OF AN ANIMAL LOVER

I woke up and got ready for the pet shop. You know what it feels like when you're really excited. I *love* animals and we were off to buy a new pet rabbit. I was dreaming of a cute, cuddly, black bundle that would play with me and be my friend.

When we arrived I saw a variety of rabbits. There were lion head and dwarf rabbits, lop eared ones and then my eyes were caught by a jet-black ball, lying down all alone. To my surprise Mum really liked him, and said we could give him a good home.
'Put him in the middle of you and Giles,' Mum said as we got into the car.

As he settled in the car, he snuggled up at the bottom of the box. As soon as we got home I opened the box as if it was a Christmas present and put him in the utility room with Monty, my guinea pig. We decided to keep the name he'd been given at the pet shop - Thumper!

I went upstairs to my room and slipped into some old and tatty clothes. I rushed downstairs and went into the utility room and calmed down Thumper with Monty. He sniffed all over the place at first, but got used to it after a while. This was the first of the many happy days of my life with my rabbit Thumper.

Lucinda Mawdsley (9)
Sunnymede School

A DAY IN THE LIFE OF A PENCIL CASE

It was the evening before school - a very hectic evening with pencils being sharpened, rulers banging, pens being filled and everything being labelled. Then I was filled with pens, pencils, colours and other equipment. Then it seemed as though the lights went out. Where am I? I thought. Then the lid flapped open and I was in Stephanie's school bag.

Light shone into the bag. On top of me were a bag of crisps, a bottle of juice and Stephanie's work book. 'Ow,' bang on my mouth fell her orange juice. As Stephanie was walking to the car her mum said, 'Let's take a picture,' so Stephanie threw me and the bag into the boot of the car and her drink leaked all over me, I was covered in wet orange juice. As I arrived at school, the bag was hung on a peg. I was taken out and placed in a desk. Around me were books, a folder and another thing I couldn't quite make out, but before the lid could be closed, a hand grabbed me and I was thrown across to the other side of the room. A boy caught me, zipped me open and took out all my insides. I was then dropped on the floor.

I felt lonely and unloved. But not for long. I was kicked down the corridor, shot under a cupboard and never seen again. Peace at last.

Sarah Gregg (9)
Sunnymede School

A DAY IN THE LIFE OF AN ELEPHANT

Hi! My name is Barney. I live along the river with my baby brother, Harry. Harry is very noisy as well as small and is always getting into trouble. One day last week he had a really *bad* day.

The first thing he did was, decide to go for a cool off in the river, but instead of wading in from the shallow, sandy beach, he decided to jump straight off a rock into the deepest pool. Water was tumbling back on him from the rocks above, and since he hadn't learnt how to swim properly, he nearly drowned. Luckily, I heard the commotion and ran and jumped in after him. I was hot as I struggled getting hold of him. I managed to get hold of his tail and dragged him out and pulled him home. Mum was angry and suspicious that I dared him to jump. But I knew I hadn't told him to jump. He was grounded for two days.

Three days later it was my aunty's birthday. When we were there, Harry went away somewhere. Then, later, we had the buffet, and there was no food. Harry came back as fat as ever. Everyone went home angry and disappointed. At home Harry was sent to bed with no food. And now I'm going to a friend's birthday party. See you later!

Edward Aleotti (10)
Sunnymede School

A Day In The Life Of A Skateboarder

This is the final day of the skateboard fanatic competition. Harry Johnson is currently in third place and getting higher marks each time. We are up to the last three rounds, if Harry Johnson wins his next two rounds he will go into the final. The rules are simple, one judge with marks out of ten, five minutes to do tricks.

The match started and Harry was skating well. He started off with a 360 and then a nose-grind. He was using plenty of good tricks and finished with a tailgrind. The five minutes were over, Harry scored seven out of ten. His opponent, on the other hand, scored six.

But Harry's next round was harder. His opponent went first and used brilliant skill to get eight and a half. Harry went next, he also used good skill on the board. This was it, whoever wins will go into the final which will be a race. The judge had made his decision, he turned the card over that said Nine. Harry had won, he was into the race. His opponent was Sean Stean.

Harry was nervous. This was live on 'Extremesport'. At the sound of the starting pistol, they went straight down a hill. Harry heard something on his board. His back wheels came off. Harry fell to the floor leaving Sean to win.

Louis Leefe (11)
Sunnymede School

A Day In The Life Of My Mum

6.45am, alarm goes and I drag myself out of bed and stumble down the stairs and let out the dogs. I put on my wellies and trundle down the drive with the dogs trotting after me.

7.00am, I bring a cup of tea up for Stewart who just grumbles and rolls over. Into Harriet's room and she's fresh out of the shower. But now I'm going where angels fear to tread, Lewis' room. Last night was a late night and after a late night he's like a bear with a sore toe.

8.00am, after I wrestled Lewis out of bed, we had breakfast and bundled into the car. Finally I dropped off the kids, that was quite a long morning.

9.03am, I've done the kids' beds and I'm on the way to work and I'm very late. At work I was there for about one hour and took some papers back with me to do tomorrow.

3.30pm, it's getting late now, so I'm going to drive back and pick up Lewis.

6.45pm, after picking up Lewis we went to Safeway and had a cup of tea, then went to get Harriet. Dinner's nearly ready so I better get it off the stove.

7.00pm, Stewart's not home yet, but he should be, he's probably staying late at the office and I've got to do some ironing and there's a huge pile of it in the wash room. The kids are watching TV.

8.00pm, Stewart came home at 7.30 and I'm so tired it's not true.

Harriet Houlgrave (11)
Sunnymede School

A Day In The Life Of A Big Sister

It's not fair. No one asked me if I'd like a little sister, especially one like Angela.

She's five years old with curly blonde hair and big brown eyes which she uses to twist Mum and Dad round her little finger. In fact, the whole family go crazy over her, but they don't know what she's really like.

So here I am walking along by the canal because Angela has again won the argument. She insisted on me taking her for a walk so she can try out her new bike. I didn't want to go, but oh no, little Miss Perfect must get her own way. There's a lady walking her golden retriever towards us. I think nothing of it until I realise that Angela is going to pedal into them. I grab her shoulder just in time as the dog jumps back in fright.

'I'm sorry,' I mumble. 'She's such a pest sometimes.' I look down, 'Is he your dog?'
'She,' the lady corrected. 'No, this is Sugar from the dogs' home.'

We chat for a while, then she asks, 'Would you like to do some dog walking? It's voluntary, but good fun.'
'Yes please!' Excellent, a chance to get away from the brat.

At home I realise that if Angela hadn't almost pedalled into that dog, I wouldn't have my new after-school job. I smile at Angela as she plays with her Barbies on the carpet and decide to take her for bike rides more often.

As she runs off to snitch to Mum that I didn't take my shoes off before I came in, I think, well, she's no angel, but she is my little sister.

Jenny McCarten (11)
Vernon Junior School

LEO

One day a woman phoned the RSPCA. She was complaining about the barking coming from her next door neighbour's house. The RSPCA came to investigate and they broke into the house. When they opened the door they couldn't believe their eyes! There were two poodles with tangled fur and a Pekinese in an even worse state. No one knew what the dogs were called.

The house was in a totally disgraceful mess. The poor dogs had been drinking out of the fish tank and even the toilet! They had been eating anything they could find. There was dog poop all around the house. They were very frightened. The RSPCA took the dogs to the Animal Hospital where all their fur had to be shaved off.

Around the same time a lady phoned the RSPCA to ask whether there were any small dogs that needed a home and the RSPCA said that there was one Pekinese and the lady, named Hilda, said, 'Well, I've got a Pekinese already called Mitzi so that would be great. It would be good company for her. I'll take him.'

After a week the RSPCA came to check out Hilda's home and said it was great for the little dog. After a while, the Pekinese got used to the new home. His fur was beginning to grow back. Hilda named the Pekinese Leo, and he was getting along just great with Mitzi as well. Leo had a broken jaw that can never be fixed but he can eat fine and loves to do it!

Alicia McCluckie (10)
Vernon Junior School

A DAY IN THE LIFE OF A SHEEP

Dear Jimmy,
When I woke up, some peculiar white things fell from the sky. Some funny looking person who was wearing white sheets walked my way. They had a walking stick in their hand. I hadn't the foggiest what they would do to me but I was prepared for a long, hard bite.

Dear Jimmy,
I just had the coolest lunch ever. Everyone's been acting really weird today. They're hanging things on my favourite tree. I got a box I can't open (they call that a present).

Dear Jimmy,
I had a posh dinner. When I went back outside, there were three weirdos talking to my enemy (with the walking stick). I feel guilty about listening in, but I couldn't help it. I heard this: 'Hello most honourable keeper of fine, fine sheep. We wise men are looking for Bethlehem.'
'Who you callin' wise mate? Have you tried lookin' in Jerusalem, not Canada? Only jokin', I were just puttin' you off. Just foller that lil' thin' up there.'
I looked up to find a blinding light.
'May thy father bless thou soul.'
Finally, I thought, they've stopped yapping.

Dear Jimmy,
I saw a fat man with a stupid beard and red clothes on the roof. He had just got off his reindeer (how can that poor little creature take his weight? Must be a miracle). Then the gigantic lunatic attempted to climb down the chimney, which is about 1/32 the size of the elephant. The light is annoying me like hell.

Sahana Krishnan (10)
Weaver Primary School

A DAY IN THE LIFE OF A VACUUM CLEANER MAKER

5.00am, *Bbbrriinnggg.* There goes my alarm. *Damn* thing, got it free with my vacuum company.

5.30am, Yes, I am proud to say I belong to a vacuum company. I put the parts in that are 2mm long. I love 'em. The vacuum cleaners that is. My girlfriend's name is Sylvia Dyson. There are pictures of vacuums everywhere in me flat.

6.00am, Makin' me cheese butties.

7.00am, Arrived at work. Guess what? I'm going to run the conveyor belts. Sammy Briggs is off and various friends will be jealous of me.

7.30am, How d'you work the damn things?

7.35am, 'What the blazes d'you think you're doing, the vacuums are going past every five seconds.'

7.40am, 'I didn't ask for them to go past every five seconds.'

8.00am, Finally got it working.

9.00am, Two hours early, coffee, I think. 'Okay guys, coffee break.'

9.09am, 'Okay guys, coffee break over.'

10.00am, Click, one vacuum done, click, two vacuums done, click . . .

10.10am, *Yawn.*

10.11am, Oops, must have dozed off for a minute.

10.15am, 'Bailey get your foot off the controls,' I told him.

10.16am, Now the belt is running at 60mph. Oops, missed one, oops, missed two.

10.17am, I'm running down the belt at top speed. I'm so out of breath.

10.30am, I've put the parts in two vacuums.

10.45am, I'm running through the black, plastic strips.

11.00am, Peter Skinner turned off the belt.

12.00, Lunch time. 'Let's eat on the belt guys.'

12.15pm, Nooo! I've turned the controls on with my feet. There goes Luke's tomato paste sandwich. Yuck!

12.30pm, *Zzzzzz . . .*

12.45pm, It's dark inside a vacuum!

Sophie Hardy (10)
Weaver Primary School

A Day In The Life Of A Guide Dog

7.30am: my mistress wakes up.

8.00am: my favourite time of the day, my mistress gives me my breakfast.

9.30am: after tidying the kitchen, we set off for a walk.

10.00am: we return home and have a drink and a biscuit together.

11.00am: the mistress goes upstairs to make the beds then she does some housework.

12.00: the mistress makes some lunch for both of us.

12.30pm: the mistress falls asleep and I lie on the rug and doze for an hour.

1.30pm: time for my second walk of the day, we stayed at the park for three hours, me racing around like a loony and my mistress sitting quietly on the bench.

4.30pm: the mistress and I walk back home for tea.

5.00pm: the mistress makes me some food and she has a cup of tea.

5.30pm: the mistress lets me jump on her lap and she strokes me under the chin.

7.00pm: the mistress lets me out in the garden for a run.

9.00pm: I help the mistress to get ready for bed.

9.30pm: the mistress and I go to bed.

Amy Thorley (11)
Weaver Primary School

A DAY IN THE LIFE OF AN ANT

10.00am - I stroll to the rock, very long way, nearly seventy-five centimetres, very tired by the end, it's not fair!

10.30am - As I was strolling back from the rock, a branch nearly fell on me - what a close one!

11.05am - I *finally* made it back from the rock, but I fell in a puddle, so okay, I live a dangerous life, I know. When I fell into the puddle, my back leg was ripped off, why does it always happen to me?

12.35pm - I hobbled to the vet and I got a new leg, but it was off a red ant, so I now have one red and three black legs. *Aaahhh!*

1.30pm - For lunch I chomped up one whole piece of grass. I actually ate it all up, wow! But now I feel sick.

2.00pm - Yawn - I am now taking a nap.

3.10pm - The queen of ants specifies we need to take two walks a day and I have only taken one so I am going to take yet another adventure in the garden.

3.15pm - I'm ready - here I go!

3.17pm - Trekking through all these flowers, what a gigantic jungle it is.

3.20pm - Nearly got eaten up by a crawling daddy long legs, but just managed to squirm into the undergrowth . . . *phew*.

3.59pm - Is that what I think it is? No, it's not a grass snake, it's a worm!

5.59pm - I'm getting ever so tired! That was one day. Imagine what tomorrow will bring! Our life is not easy!

Heather Crane (11)
Weaver Primary School

A Day In The Life Of Shane, Westlife

Dear Diary,

Woke up *really* late this morning, I forgot to set my alarm, just so stupid of me.

You should have seen the traffic I was in; it was just so typical. I was stuck behind two blinking lorries, there was a very long queue, it was about five miles long.

Eventually I got to work, I was only two hours late, and the boss had a right go at me for being *so* late. By now it was 7.00am and I hadn't started to rehearse my song which was called 'I Have A Dream'. When I got there the rest of the boys were already dressed up, ready to go and rehearse the song. It took me half an hour to get ready.

'Right you miserable lot, let's get on with rehearsing this show!' shouted the boss.
'I don't even know the words,' I said.
'Well we do,' said the rest of the boys.
'What do you mean you've got the words? Why haven't I got the words?' I proclaimed.
'You haven't got the words because they were given to us when you were stuck in traffic!'

A few hours passed, it was nearly time to perform to the audience.

'Yawnnnnnnn. I'm so tired, I feel like going to bed.'
'No, you cannot fall asleep now, we are just about to perform.'

I managed to keep awake all night, now I'm at home getting ready for bed and I'm ready to fall asleep! Zzzzzz.

Amy-Beth Perry (11)
Weaver Primary School

A Day In The Life Of My Dad

6.45am. Just woke up, still half asleep. Oh! It's Monday morning, at least I'm not on call.

6.50am. Heading up for the bathroom.

7.00am. Heading downstairs to make a cuppa, for everyone.

7.07am. Rushing for the toilet, *oh no!* Someone's in, *hurry up!*

7.07.30am. Still waiting!

7.08am. Still waiting!

7.09am. Still waiting!

7.10am. Still waiting!

7.15am. Ah, that's better.

7.30am. Hurry up kids!

7.45am. I'm meant to set off for work now.

7.50am. I'm late for work!

8.00am. Just switched on my computer and looking at blood results, this one's not good.

8.30am. Bit stuck on paper work and still behind schedule.

8.35am. Anita brings in coffee.

8.45am. First patient just walked in, with bad headache.

8.50am. I feel a headache coming on.

9.00am. Just popped off to the toilet.

9.15am. Coming out of the bathroom and just seen loads of people standing outside my room.

9.20am. Time for a cup of tea. 'Anita, another one please.'

9.30am. Patient just walked in with sore arm. (More work getting done now.) Seeing lots of patients with not much wrong with them.

10.30am. The third patient to walk in with a cold.

10.40am. Time for another brew, 'Anita, please.'

11.15am. Someone just walked in with a red rash all over his face.

11.30am. Surgery finished, *hooray*, just three visits left.

11.35am. Or I'm a bit itchy, I hope I haven't caught anything.

1.00pm. Off home for a quick lunch, can't wait for my beef butty and Scrumpy Jack.

2.30pm. More paperwork before minor surgery list.

3.00pm - 5.00pm. Removed three moles, two lumps, two fingernails and a pussy, smelly cyst.

Cora Hamdy (10)
Weaver Primary School

AND WHO SAYS FISH HAVE NO MEMORY?

9.01am. I swim into a large green and white thing. It's hard with a bumpy surface. Hey look, there's a hole at the other end and I can swim through! It's very dark in here. There's a light at the other end. Oh! There's somebody else here now! His name is probably 'Fish' like mine.

'Hey Fish, look, there's stuff coming from the heavens! I was hungry. Yum, this is tasty.

Fish! Hide in this hole I discovered earlier! There's a creature outside. Can you see its eyes? They're as quick as fleas. It's all hairy with four legs and a long, thin, extra piece of fur at the back.'

It's trying to put its large fin into the bowl. It has bits of broken glass on the end of it! I'm frightened . . .

'Oh, don't worry, Fish, something even bigger has taken it away! I hope it's friendly. I has even longer bits of glass on the end of its fins and they're painted red!'

And who says fish have no memory?

9.06am. I swim into large green and white thing. It's hard with a bumpy surface.

Hey look, there's a hole I can swim through! It's very dark in here . . .

And who says?

Edward Charlton (10)
Weaver Primary School

A Day In The Life Of A Dentist

Boy, the roads were awful this morning. There was one distinguished dipstick in front of me! The road was windy - no way of overtaking him. Typical men drivers! By the time I'd finally parked my car I was half an hour late. The boss was going to kill me.

Very quickly swipe on my gloves and drape - get my tools ready, and in comes ex-boyfriend Peter - a rather big jerk! Next I've got sweet Jessica and her mother, lovely people. The problem is they never clean their teeth. There's lots of tooth decay, last night's tea and sickly brown choppers. Yuck!

I had all my regulars this morning - quite a few old geezers! And only one set of sparkling white teeth in sight. Mine!

I've got the holey Wallace now. This man is in his fifties, has sixty-two fillings and he needs his teeth cleaned by me once a month. Otherwise this old Wallace is a very friendly, law abiding, cantankerous old man! He also has this great big chunk of grey, spiky hair upon his head.

Next I'm faced with Vicky - the town snob. Her front teeth are glistening white but the back ones are spotty yellow and black with false gold fillings. Today, she wants me to put a brace on because it's the fashion. Sad!

Finally a day's hectic work finished and as I stumble over to my car after a lecture from the boss man, I find that my car's been clamped. I parked it in the town Mayor's spot!

Looking forward to a night's sleep in my car, not!

Anna Wallace (11)
Weaver Primary School

A Day In The Life Of A Cat

Hi, I'm Cuddle the Cat, half the time of my life I'm a house cat and the other half of my life I'm an alley cat. My house address is 416 Flee Street. My alley address is 2 Dustbin Alley because it is always full of dustbins. At night it's really fun because I sneak out of the cat flap and go to the Alley, but anyway, let's get back to the story. When I am at the Alley I invite some good friends of mine to the house for a party because at my house on Flee Street it is so boring, we hardly ever do anything. My friend Freddie is so fat he can't ever fit through the cat flap, so we call him Fatso. He said he was going to go on a diet but that promise never came true. He still has to come through the back door. At the party we have the music on full blast, but the family never wake up, the only person that does is Jim the baby. After the party I go back in the cat play area. As I am a talking cat I play pranks on people, for example, if people are walking down the street when I'm on the way to the Alley, I say 'You're a freak,' then I hide. The people then turn around and expect to see the people that said it.

One day I was so naughty I pressed a button on the phone when someone was on it, disconnecting them. There is a girl the family named Melissa who I really like. My owners split up and one of them moved house. Me and Melissa and the rest of the family went to see him at the new house.
The man owner named Christopher said, 'I really like it and I am really pleased with it.'
I just said I hated it but only Melissa knows I can talk.
Then Christopher asked, 'Did the cat just talk?'
Melissa replied, 'No!'
After we had lunch we went home from the house that I hated.

So there you go, I've told you a day in the life of a cat or maybe a few days in the life of a cat but that's not important right now. What is important is that being a cat I have nine lives, so I'll be back to tell you many more days in the lives of a cat!

Rose Marshall (9)
Yew Tree Primary School

A DAY IN THE LIFE OF A COW

Hi there moo buddies! My name is Clarissa the cow and I live at Buckingham Farm. I don't do much at all during the day, just like the rest of my family. I say moo a lot though. I'd say Mum was the busiest of all us cows.

In the morning I wake up and eat delicious green grass for my breakfast, and then I play with my brothers and sisters. I say, 'Moo,' to my friends in the next field. My mum, Clair, is so busy twice a day being milked by farmer Lizzie. I'll be milked when I get older. I can't wait. It's so important to be milked. Mum loves being milked.

At night I sleep in a barn. It's dark and quite spooky. My eldest sister, Chloe, is always kicking me with her back leg and it hurts. When I tell her not to kick me, she just moos under her breath. My younger brother, Charlie, just sleeps all the time. He never says moo.

My father is called Carl. He eats grass and that's it. My father is kind but he never says much, just the odd moo now and again, if we get in his way.

I love sunny days in the fields, but hate the winter when I have to stay in all the time. It gets cold and I never get to say moo as much as I want to.

So I've told you about my family and a day in the life of a cow, so boring, don't you think?

Bye, bye, moo buddies!

Lucy Counter (9)
Yew Tree Primary School